Bubba to the Rescue

By Jennifer Walker

Guinevere,
Keep up the good
work in the
Friendship Club!
Liz Walk
July 2012

D1441291

Bubba to the Rescue
Book Two: Green Meadow Riders
Author: Jennifer Walker

ISBN-13: 978-0984209569
ISBN-10: 0984209565

SAN 858-737X

10 9 8 7 6 5 4 3 2 1

Editor: Michelle Devon
Illustrator / Artwork: Debra Torrico
Cover: Accentuate Author Services

www.authorjennwalker.com/bubba.html
www.TwinTrinityBooks.com

Published in the United States.

Table of Contents

Chapter One: *A New Beginning* 1

Chapter Two: *The Fire* 5

Chapter Three: *Fight for your Life!* 13

Chapter Four: *Clean Up* 30

Chapter Five: *Moving Day* 51

Chapter Six: *Spark* 65

Chapter Seven: *Halloween* 79

Chapter Eight: *November* 99

Chapter Nine: *Christmas Formal* 115

Chapter Ten: *The Dance* 133

Chapter Eleven: *Resolution* 147

Chapter Twelve: *The Schooling Show* 165

Chapter Thirteen: *Nancy Miller* 183

Chapter Fourteen: *Christmas* 197

Chapter Fifteen: *Court Order* 213

Chapter Sixteen: *New Horse* 227

Chapter Seventeen: *Show Season* 233

Chapter One:
A New Beginning

"Do you, Dan Clark, take this woman, Helen Green to be your lawfully wedded wife, in sickness and in health, till death do you part?"

Leslie shivered slightly. Goose bumps ran up and down her arm when the preacher said the words, and her eyes filled.

I can't believe this is happening, she thought. *It's like a dream come true!*

She studied her father's face when he said, "I do." His eyes sparkled, fixed on Helen's. Leslie had the feeling that she and the other hundred or so people in the church were like the audience at a movie, where the characters were in their own world, not knowing they were being watched.

"Do you, Helen Green, take this man to be your lawfully wedded husband, in sickness and in health, as long as you both shall live?"

Leslie's cheeks ached from smiling. *I don't think I've stopped smiling for one second in the past three months, ever since Dad asked her to marry him.* She almost giggled at the thought.

She wished she could see Helen's face when she said, "I do," but all she could see was the back of her head and the look of pure joy on her father's face. Leslie quickly wiped the tear that escaped from her right eye and trickled down her cheek. She hoped nobody would notice.

She looked over her left shoulder and saw her boyfriend, Alex, in the third row. Her smile grew just a little bigger, which she hadn't thought possible, when he winked at her.

He's so handsome in his suit. I wish he'd dress like that all the time!

"Then by the power vested in me by the state of California, I now pronounce you Husband and Wife. You may kiss the bride."

The church erupted in applause and several more tears made their way down Leslie's cheeks while she watched her father kiss his new wife — her new stepmother. She thought briefly of her birth mother, who had died when Leslie was ten, and directed her eyes up to look at the vaulted ceiling above her.

Mom, if you're up there, I hope you're happy for Dad and me. I think you would want this for us. You know I'll never forget you, even if I call her Mom.

Leslie was brought out of her silent prayer when Helen turned to give her a hug.

"Welcome to the family, Helen," she choked out, unable to control the tears of joy.

"I can't imagine anywhere else I'd rather be or anyone else I'd want to be there with," Helen whispered, her voice thick with emotion.

Leslie's father joined them in their hug, and the three

stood together for a moment before the preacher cleared his throat.

"Ready?" Dan asked. Leslie and Helen nodded, breaking their hold and wiping their eyes. The three linked arms and turned to face their friends and family.

"Ladies and gentlemen," the preacher said, "I present, for the first time, Mr. and Mrs. Dan Clark and their daughter Leslie."

The applause was deafening when Leslie and her parents walked down the aisle together, arm in arm. Once outside in the bright sunshine, the three turned to face each other again.

"Well, girls, this is the beginning of a whole new life for us. Are you ready for it?"

"I'm ready for anything!" Leslie said.

"I wouldn't want it any other way," Helen said, and she smiled.

Chapter Two:
The Fire

"Are you ready yet, Leslie?" Alex's voice sounded impatient.

Leslie gave herself a little mental shake. She realized she'd been staring at her saddle for several minutes when she was supposed to be tacking up. Alex, Leslie's boyfriend, was ready, holding the reins of a completely tacked Fred, one of Helen's lesson horses. He looked at her, crossing his arms and tapping his foot.

"Yes, sorry. I was just thinking about Dad and Helen on their honeymoon. I wonder how they're doing?"

"I'm sure they're having a great time. It was nice of the Browns to let them use their cabin in the woods so they could have a nice trip."

The Browns were clients of Helen, who was a horse trainer and the owner of Green Meadow Training Stables. The Browns had once allowed Leslie to show one of their horses, Charlie, before they sold him.

Leslie grabbed her bridle off a nearby hook. "Yes, that was generous of them. I'm sure you're right; they probably are having a wonderful time. Dad almost never gets to go on vacation, and I don't know if Helen has ever taken one, so this is really a great chance for them."

She unclipped the cross ties from Lucky's halter and unbuckled it so she could slip it off his nose and buckle it around his neck while she put on his bridle. Lucky was her horse, an Arabian gelding she'd bought at the livestock auction the spring before. His previous owners had abandoned him because they didn't think he was good enough to represent their breeding program, but Leslie believed in him and won a National Championship with him. Despite Lucky's success as a show horse, Leslie's father insisted on calling him Bubba.

When every buckle was in place, Leslie said, "All right. I'm ready. Let's go!"

They led their horses outside, waving goodbye to the assistant trainer, Julie, who was riding a horse in the indoor arena. They grabbed their helmets off their hooks as they passed and strapped them on while they walked. Once outside, they double checked to make sure the girths were tight, then mounted and turned their horses' noses toward the woods.

"It's been a long time since we've been on a trail ride," Alex said.

"I know. I think the last time was the barn trail ride last spring."

"Oh, yeah! Isn't that when Cindy's pony ran away with her?"

Leslie and Lucky had saved the day when a young rider had mounted her pony, against orders and without permission, and the pony took off toward home. Leslie and Lucky were able to catch up with them and stop the pony before the girl was hurt.

Leslie nodded. "Yep. Let's hope this ride is much less eventful!"

They rode in silence for a few minutes, following the easy path through the woods that covered a portion of the Green Meadows property. Helen's riders had permission to ride on neighboring properties as well, so they had access to several miles of trails. Leslie had promised Julie they would only be gone for a couple of hours, so she knew she would need to keep track of the time.

While they rode, a strong breeze made Leslie's pony-tail dance and blew tendrils of hair across her face.

"What's that smell?" she asked, sniffing the wind.

"I'm not sure," Alex answered. "It smells familiar, but it's so faint I can't quite make it out."

Their trail took a turn to the east, and Leslie realized what she had smelled when she saw a thick plume of smoke rising above the trees. Her stomach clenched; forest fires could be scary and dangerous things.

"Uh oh, do you see that?" She pointed.

"I sure do, and it doesn't look very far away. Do you think it could be over by the Bakers' place?"

"Hard to say," Leslie answered with a worried frown. "But they have that old wooden barn. It's like a big pile of kindling—do you think we should go make sure they're OK?"

Alex's eyes were round with alarm and his skin had gone pale, causing his freckles to stand out. "I have a pretty bad feeling about this, Leslie. It's Wednesday afternoon, so the Bakers are probably at work. I don't know if there's anyone home to get the horses out if the fire reaches the barn."

Leslie's heart leapt into her throat, but she knew she and Alex were the only hope those horses might have if what Alex feared were true.

"We'd better hurry. Come on, Lucky!"

She squeezed Lucky's sides and leaned forward, and he leapt into a canter, Alex and Fred right beside them.

Leslie and Alex galloped through the woods with their horses, eyes strained ahead to watch for hazards in the trail, such as rocks, holes and low branches.

Leslie caught glimpses of the ever-thickening column of smoke. The smell of smoke in the air grew stronger, and a few bits of ash floated down around them. Leslie felt nauseated with fear, but she pushed Lucky to run faster. The thought of the Bakers' eight horses trapped in a burning barn pushed all thoughts for her own safety out of her head.

When they emerged from the woods and turned down a service road on the Bakers' property, they could see the flames licking the sky just a few hundred yards behind the rickety old barn. The property was surround-ed by trees, and Leslie had learned at school that the dry grass that covered much of it would provide ready fuel for the fire.

"Can you see the driveway?" Alex asked. Leslie could barely hear him, even though he shouted over the sound of pounding hooves.

"I think it's over there," Leslie shouted back, pointing toward the house and the main driveway. "Looks like the whole road is on fire!"

"They'll never be able to get in. We'd better do some-thing, and fast!"

"Let's turn the sprinklers on in the arena and put the horses in there. The footing is sand, so they should be safe."

"Good idea. You go turn them on and open the gate,

and I'll start pulling the horses out of the barn."

When they reached the arena, they jumped off their horses and tied them to the fence. Leslie cringed at having to tie them with their reins since they could hurt their mouths if they got scared and pulled back, but she didn't see any other way. Alex ran to the barn while she ran around the perimeter of the fence until she found the valve to turn on the sprinklers. Once they were on, she ran to the barn to help Alex.

Thankfully, each horse had a halter and lead rope hanging by their stall. Leslie and Alex worked quickly to halter the horses and lead them out, each leading two at a time, to the arena where the sprinklers and lack of fuel would keep them safe from the fire. Some of the horses balked at going into the arena with the spraying water, but Alex and Leslie led them with a firm hand and encouraging words, and eventually they got them all into the enclosure. While they worked, bits of ash fell around them. The sky, which had been blue when they left the ranch, was completely grey.

When Alex latched the gate after the last horse was safely inside, Lucky snorted and whinnied. He and Fred arched their necks and danced, eyes large and round with fear.

"We'd better get out of here, Leslie. That fire is getting really close!" Alex grabbed Leslie and pulled her with him toward their horses. She ran to keep up.

By the time they untied and mounted their horses, the fire had reached the barn. Between the hay stacked inside and the dry old wood, Leslie knew it would not be long before it was completely engulfed in flames. She and Alex kicked their mounts into a gallop and headed back toward Green Meadow.

The air around them was thick with smoke by that time, and Leslie's throat burned from her efforts. She coughed over and over again, and she could faintly hear Alex doing the same. She tried to put her discomfort out of her mind so she could concentrate on getting through the woods and back home before the fire reached them.

While they ran, Leslie could hear the horses calling frantically in the arena behind her. "Do you think they'll be OK?" She shouted to Alex.

"It's far enough from the barn they won't be in danger there, and since there's no dry grass around it, they should be fine," he yelled back.

Leslie took her eyes off the trail to look at his face. It was covered in grime. His brows were furrowed in worry. She imagined her own face looked much like his.

"We can't worry about them anymore, Leslie. We have to get home and make sure Green Meadow is safe. If we wait any longer, we could be trapped."

Leslie's stomach lurched; she knew he was right. She looked back over her shoulder and could see flashes of orange through the trees. She pushed Lucky to go even faster, although his breathing was labored and his neck was soaked with sweat and covered in froth where the reins rubbed it.

"Lucky, I'm so sorry, but we have to keep going," she breathed into his mane. "I promise, if you just get us home, you can have a nice, long rest."

Silently, she prayed to God to get them home safely.

While they ran, Leslie could hear the roar of the fire grow louder, accompanied by the pops of sparks and the breaking of branches. She could feel the heat increase on her back and knew it was getting closer.

They were almost to the property line for Green

Meadow when they heard a crashing in the underbrush to their left. Lucky and Fred jumped to the side, stopping to whirl and face the brush. Leslie nearly lost her seat, but she clung to Lucky's mane and managed to hang on. She looked up, and a horse leapt out of the bushes. Its eyes and nostrils were large and veins stood out on its neck.

Lucky snorted, his eyes large as he stared at the strange horse. Leslie could feel him trembling beneath her, so she stroked his neck and told him, "You're OK, Lucky. It's just a horse." Her voice sounded shaky and strained to her own ears.

"Whose horse is that?" Alex asked. His voice sounded as shaky as hers.

Leslie did not have time to answer, because a tree branch fell behind them in a shower of sparks. Beneath her, Lucky screamed and bolted forward.

Alex and Leslie run through the burning forest.

Chapter Three:
Fight for your Life!

Leslie clung to Lucky's mane and lay as low across his neck as she could. Her lungs burned, and the smoke in the air was so thick she could barely breathe. Her eyes stung, and tears coursed down her face. She buried her face in Lucky's mane and silently prayed he would not step in a hole or trip on a rock. The sound of the roaring fire, crashing trees and galloping hooves filled her ears.

Then, time seemed to stand still.

With her eyes closed, the deafening noise around her faded until all she could hear was the beating of Lucky's heart. She felt numb, barely aware of anything around her except the horse between her knees. She did not know where Alex and Fred were or the mysterious horse that had jumped out of the bushes. All she was aware of in the world was Lucky and darkness.

She did not know how long she floated along in that dream world, but she was brought out of it abruptly when a spark landed on her back, sending searing pain through her skin. The blazing heat and roaring of the fire and the beat of the galloping hooves came rushing back in a torrent. Lucky screamed and ran even faster, and she guessed he had been hit by a spark too. Leslie was afraid to open her eyes, knowing the fire was practically on top of them.

If we don't get to Green Meadow soon, we're not going to make it. She thought desperately. *We have to get there!*

Only seconds later, Leslie felt a new sensation: water. They had reached Green Meadow, and the sprinklers were on. She opened her stinging eyes and nearly cried with relief. The fire had halted its march at the edge of the trees behind her, held back by the lush green grass and the high-powered sprinklers. Most importantly, Alex and Fred were on one side of her, the stray horse on the other.

In the pastures around them, horses ran around in alarm. Leslie knew they would be safe from the fire, since the fencing was fire retardant and the wet, green grass would keep the fire away, but she felt sorry for them in their fear. She and Alex were nearing the barn, so she sat back in her saddle and pulled on the reins, calling for Lucky to slow. She could see there were several people around the barn, house and various outbuildings with hoses, watering down the roofs and walls to protect them from stray sparks.

Julie ran out through the barn doors with a halter and lead rope in her hands.

"Thank God you're all right!" she exclaimed when they pulled to a stop in front of her. "Whose horse is this?"

She put the halter behind her back and walked slowly toward the stray horse with her free hand stretched out for him to sniff.

"We don't know," Leslie said while she dismounted.

Lucky's head drooped and his breath came in ragged bursts, his sides rising and falling alarmingly. She clucked at him and led him in a circle at the walk so his muscles wouldn't tie up.

"He caught up with us in the forest and followed us."

The strange horse dripped with sweat, and he was breathing as hard as Lucky. He did not protest or try to move away when Julie softly walked closer, brought the halter out from behind her back and gently slipped it over his nose and buckled it behind his ears.

"I wonder if he belongs to the Bakers," she said, following Leslie in the circle.

"I don't think so," Alex put in. He had also dismounted and walked beside Fred, whose breathing was as labored as the other two horses. "We went there when we saw the smoke and put their horses in the arena with the sprinklers on so they would be safe. The road looked like it was blocked by the fire, so I don't know when the Bakers will be able to get to them."

His face was nearly black with soot, broken only by the rivulets of sweat that ran down it. Leslie put her hand to her face and felt the same mixture of grime.

Julie stopped and stared at them. "You ran all the way from the Bakers'?" she asked.

Leslie nodded.

"Well, that was a very brave thing you did, but now we need to take care of Green Meadow. Untack your horses and let's put all three of them in the indoor arena. That way, they'll move around until they cool off. I don't want them standing in their stalls after that long run. Alex, call your parents and tell them you're OK."

Alex and Leslie did as they were told, walking inside on shaky legs. Although her arms felt like rubber, Leslie quickly pulled her saddle off Lucky and dropped it on a nearby saddle rack. Alex did the same, and then they led their horses into the arena and pulled the bridles off to let them loose. Julie had already put the stray horse in there, so after Alex called his house and left a message about what was going on, he and Leslie went outside to see how they could help.

Leslie could hear fire engine sirens in the distance for the first time since the fire started, as well as the sound of a helicopter flying overhead. She looked at the fire that raged just a couple of hundred yards away, eating away the forest beyond the pastures. She felt a rush of sadness at the thought of losing all those old, beautiful trees. She watched while the two ranch hands dragged lengths of thick fire hose toward the forest and asked Julie what they were doing.

"They can connect to the water main out there and fight the fire," the assistant trainer responded. "There are only so many fire fighters and they can only do so much, so Juan and Josh will do what they can to help from this side."

Her brow was creased with worry, and the corners of her mouth turned down into a frown.

"Besides, I don't want you to worry, but right now there's no way for anyone to get in or out of Green Meadow. The fire spread amazingly fast and blocked off the road."

She opened her arms wide, and Leslie and Alex stepped in for a group hug. Leslie could hear Julie sniffle, and a teardrop landed in her hair.

After the terrifying flight through the woods, Leslie felt numb from fear. This last piece of bad news could do nothing to make her feel any worse, so she squeezed Julie and Alex a little tighter. She said, "It'll be OK. Right Julie? They'll put the fire out. Won't they?"

"Yeah, and this place is so wet, there's no way it's coming in here," Alex put in.

Julie sniffled again. "Yes, I'm sure we'll be all right. I was just so scared when I saw the fire spreading so fast, knowing you were out there somewhere and unable to reach you. I can't tell you how relieved I was to see you. It's all a little overwhelming."

She squeezed them tight, then released them. She wiped her eyes, gave herself a little shake, and smiled a little.

"OK, if we're going to save Green Meadow, we need to do everything we can to keep everything watered down. Can you two take those hoses over there and start spraying the roof? I'm going to close all the windows and doors to try to keep as much smoke out as possible."

Alex and Leslie nodded and ran in opposite directions to take up their positions. When Leslie reached hers, she turned on the water and trained the stream on the roof of the barn. She sprayed back and forth, walking as far as the hose let her, then sprayed the barn walls and nearby bushes and flowers. By the time she had gone as far as she could in one direction, the places she had sprayed in the other were dry from the heat and she would have to start again.

She was soaked in sweat, from both the effort of her work and the heat of the fire. Her arms ached until she thought she could no longer hold them up, but she forced herself to continue. The wind blew her ponytail into her face every few seconds, and she had to continually pull her hair out of her eyes and mouth.

After what seemed like days, Julie approached and

held out her hand for the hose. "Time to take a break, Leslie. You look like you're dead on your feet."

"Thank you, Julie, but I can manage. I wouldn't want anything to happen to Green Meadow." It was an effort for Leslie to shout over the wind. Her voice was hoarse, and her throat felt scratchy.

Julie took the hose from Leslie's hands gently, but firmly. "Go in the office and lie down, Leslie, and that's an order. Juan and Josh are doing a great job holding the fire off, and I think this will be over soon. I don't want you to collapse from heat exhaustion; your parents would never forgive me."

She put her hand on Leslie's shoulder and gave her a little push toward the barn door.

The thought of lying down was attractive, and despite the fact she wanted to stay out and help, Leslie knew she needed a rest badly. She obediently stumbled toward the office, willing her legs to carry her just a few more yards. With her adrenaline wearing off, she realized she was even more tired than she had thought. Her arms and legs felt like rubber, trembling with the effort of walking, letting herself into the barn and then the office. Once she made it inside, she took in a deep breath of the filtered air that smelled only faintly of smoke and collapsed on the couch.

Leslie did not know how long she had been asleep when Alex woke her.

"What time is it?" she asked, rubbing the sleep out of her eyes. She looked at the window and saw the world outside was dark and bolted upright. "I'd better get out and start watering again!"

"It's about eight o'clock," he answered, sitting next to her and placing one hand on hers while gently pushing stray strands of hair out of her face with the other. "The danger has passed. Juan and Josh managed to put out the fire that surrounded us, and the fire fighters cleared the road. My parents are on their way here to get me."

"They must be worried sick. I can't believe I slept through the whole thing! You and Julie and the others must be exhausted," she groaned.

"Everyone got a chance to take a break," Alex said. "But we just couldn't bear to wake you up. You were completely out every time we came in to check on you."

He smiled and winked before adding, "I guess you needed your beauty sleep after all that sweating and stuff. You were snoring and everything."

Leslie smiled back and swatted him on the arm.

"You're not supposed to say that! You're supposed to say I'm beautiful, no matter what I look like! Besides, I don't snore."

Alex said in a flat tone, as though from rote, "You're beautiful, no matter what you look like." He laughed and added in his normal tone, "Now come on, we need to check on the horses."

Leslie stood and followed him out of the office, her thoughts turning to the stray horse that had followed them home. "I wonder whose horse that is. Have you checked on him or Fred or Lucky?"

"No, there hasn't been time until now, and I knew you'd want to check Lucky yourself so I came to get you first. Julie already called the vet to come out and check them over, and she'll be here as soon as she can."

"Good idea. Let's put them in the cross ties and clean them up."

They picked up their halters from where they had left them before their trail ride, which seemed like days rather than hours before. They let themselves through the gate to the arena, but while Alex latched it behind them, Leslie froze in horror. The three horses were standing together, heads down, all-but-lifeless eyes staring straight ahead of them.

Their coats were matted with sweat, which she had expected, but that was not the extent of the evidence of their trauma. Their hair was singed all over, and there were bare places where the hair had apparently been burned off. Their legs were swollen and puffy.

Tears sprang into Leslie's eyes for what seemed like the hundredth time that day.

"Lucky!" she cried, breaking out of her trance to run forward and throw her arms around her horse's neck and bury her face in his mane. "I'm so sorry, Lucky. I didn't know this would happen to you! You were so brave, running to keep us safe even though you were hurting and scared. How could I have done this to you?"

"It's not your fault, Les," Alex's gentle voice sounded from behind her, and she felt his comforting hand on her shoulder. "The fire spread faster than anyone could have expected. We did the right thing saving the Bakers' horses, and now we just have to hope these guys come out of it OK."

Leslie sniffed and nodded; she could not have borne the thought of leaving the Bakers' horses in the barn to perish, but she was wracked with guilt over what she had done to Lucky.

What if he doesn't pull out of this? She thought. *What if he dies?*

The thought sent her into another fit of sobs, and Alex

pulled her into his arms, hugging her and stroking her back and hair.

"Sshh... come on, Leslie, these horses need us. Take a deep breath and let's see what we can do for them. Dr. Burke will be here soon, and she'll do the best she can for them, OK?"

Leslie knew he was right. Standing there crying would not help Lucky. She took a deep breath, pulled herself together and buckled Lucky's halter on his head.

"Let's lead them over to the water and see if they'll drink. I don't know if they've had any since we put them in here."

There was a water trough in the corner, but she suspected the horses had not moved from their spot by the gate since they had been put in the arena. Alex followed her with Fred, and the stray horse followed him.

The horses walked slowly on stiff legs, and Lucky limped badly on his right hind. Seeing that nearly sent Leslie into another crying fit, but she forced herself to remain calm.

I need to be brave for Lucky, she reminded herself.

She let Lucky pick the pace, talking to him in gentle and encouraging tones. "Come on, Lucky, you can do it. Just a little bit further. I bet you're thirsty, aren't you?"

She could hear Alex murmuring similar things to Fred, and she smiled despite her grief.

He's really becoming quite the horseman, she thought.

After a painstaking couple of minutes, they reached the water trough and the horses drank eagerly. It was just large enough for all three of them to put their muzzles in. Alex and Leslie had to press themselves against the arena fence to give the horses room.

"Good thinking, Leslie. Look how thirsty they are."

He reached across and turned on the spigot to refill the trough, and the horses did not even flinch when the water poured out of the spout.

After allowing them to drink their fill, Alex and Leslie turned to make their way slowly back across the arena to the gate and the cross tie area. Leslie looked into Lucky's eyes and saw that a little of the life had returned to them, but they still looked dull.

He must be in a lot of pain, she thought. *It's a good thing Dr. Burke will be here soon.*

The veterinarian was backing her truck through the large open barn door by the time all three horses were in the cross ties. Leslie admired Dr. Burke's efficient, professional movements while the veterinarian quickly opened the compartments on the back of her truck, pulling out supplies and putting on rubber gloves.

While she worked, Dr. Burke said, "Well, I understand you two are the heroes who saved the Bakers' horses. They were worried sick when they couldn't get into their property, and you can imagine their surprise when they finally got in and found their horses safe and sound. That was a very brave thing you did."

Leslie and Alex looked at each other and smiled, then each dropped their eyes shyly to their feet. "Julie said you had a pretty harrowing ride home, and picked up a stray along the way, so let's take a look and see what we can do for these guys."

Leslie had always liked Dr. Burke. Green Meadows's regular veterinarian had an efficient and professional manner, combined with an easy and gentle touch that put her patients and owners at ease.

Dr. Burke walked over to her patients and took a quick look at them before speaking again. "Alex, why don't you get a bucket of warm water and a very clean sponge and wipe them down to get the sweat off? Be very gentle—no soap and no hose. They look like they might be feeling a bit sore from the burns. Leslie, you can help me take a look at Lucky first. Looks like he's got a nasty wound on that back leg."

Leslie had not had a chance to look at Lucky's leg until Dr. Burke pointed it out. When she did, she felt as though a fist gripped her heart. She swayed as a wave of nausea washed over her. Not only was the leg very swollen, but there was also a burn about three inches long and a couple of inches wide right on his hock.

"A branch fell behind us. It must have hit him," she said quietly, her stomach churning. Whatever had hit him had taken off all the hair and several layers of skin. The wound was an angry red, rimmed in black.

Dr. Burke went right to work. First she gave Lucky a shot. "To ease his pain," she explained.

She instructed Leslie to run cold water on the leg to take down the swelling. "While you do that, I'll check over the rest of him. After you get the swelling to go down a bit, I'll inspect that burn more closely and see what I need to do with it."

Leslie forced herself to quell her panic and concentrate on what the doctor was telling her.

"He has quite a few minor burns, so I'll put some ointment on them and leave some with you to apply twice a day for the next few days."

Finished with her inspection of Lucky for the moment, Dr. Burke stepped away to check on Fred. Leslie grabbed the hose from its hook, turned it on to a low stream and trained it on the burn on the large joint of Lucky's back leg.

"This will put you out of commission for a while, I'm afraid," Leslie told her horse with a frown. "Looks like there will be no more showing for us this season."

She sighed; she had only bought him a few months before and amazed herself and everyone else when she and Lucky were National Champions only a short time later. She had hoped to take Lucky to one more show before winter, but the last one of the season was only two weeks away. She didn't think Lucky would recover in time.

Behind her, she heard Dr. Burke tell Alex, "Fred just has minor burns and abrasions, so I put ointment on them and he should come out of this just fine. His legs are swollen, but that's to be expected given his age and what he's been through. Hose them down with cold water like Leslie's doing, and I'll give him some Bute to help with the pain and swelling. We'll put him on antibiotics just to make sure he doesn't get an infection. We'll keep a close eye on all of them for the next few days to make sure they heal, of course. Hand walking every day, or even light riding at the walk, will help that swelling go down."

Leslie was relieved that Fred wasn't seriously hurt. He was Helen's best lesson horse, and Alex and Leslie had both spent many hours learning how to ride on him.

I can't imagine Green Meadow without him! She looked over at him fondly.

"And who is this young man?" Dr. Burke asked. Leslie saw she had stepped over to the stray horse and was looking him over. Leslie shifted so she could see what the veterinarian was doing while she still kept the water running on Lucky's hock.

"We don't know," Leslie answered. "We came upon him in the woods during the fire, and he followed us home. Do you recognize him as belonging to any of your clients?"

Dr. Burke rubbed her chin in thought while she looked at the horse. "Hm, it's hard to say. He doesn't strike me as a horse I recognize, but he's in pretty bad shape. He might have looked different the last time I worked on him."

While she spoke, she checked the horse over and put ointment on his wounds like she had with the other horses.

"It looks like he's been in the woods for a while," she went on, almost as though she were talking to herself. "His mane and tail are full of pine needles and burrs. His feet are chipped and much too long, and he's very thin. I can't tell what condition his coat was in because it's singed from the fire, but I'd be willing to bet it was pretty poor. I wouldn't be surprised if he ran away some time ago and has been fending for himself ever since."

"Have you heard any reports of missing horses?" Alex asked. "I haven't, and I haven't seen any notices on the bulletin board at the feed store."

"I don't think I have, now that you mention it," Dr. Burke answered.

"Do you think someone could have turned him loose on purpose?" Leslie asked.

The thought of doing that to a horse was terrible in her mind, but she had heard that some people did that very thing when they could no longer afford their horse and could not find a new home for it.

"It's certainly possible, although I would hate to think anyone would do that. Domestic horses are not like Mustangs. They don't survive on their own very well. The land around here doesn't have enough food for them, and domestic horses don't have the survival instincts of their wild cousins. They're used to being fed regular meals instead of finding their own."

"I would think he would be lonely out there by himself too," Leslie put in.

Alex snickered, but Dr. Burke nodded seriously. "Actually, she's right, Alex. Horses are herd animals and rely on each other for protection and companionship. They are very rarely happy living by themselves."

Alex looked at his feet and found something on the floor to scratch at with his toe while Leslie smiled triumphantly.

Leslie said, "No wonder he was so anxious to follow us and let Julie catch him. He was probably happy to be with people again, and he needed Lucky and Fred to lead him out of the fire and make him feel safe."

"I bet you're right, Leslie. OK, why don't you come over here and use that hose on Spark's legs while I take a closer look at Lucky's hock?"

Leslie smiled again. "Spark?"

"Well, he needs a name, doesn't he? Until you find his owner, anyway. I figure Spark fits him. Don't you?"

Leslie giggled. "I have to admit it does. Spark it is, then!"

She dragged the hose over to Spark and aimed the cold water at his legs. She had not examined him closely before, but once she was right next to him, she could see he was quite pretty. She could tell he was an Arabian, like Lucky and Fred, with large eyes and small ears that tipped in toward each other. His profile started with a bulge between the eyes, with a graceful dish below them that tapered to a small, elegant muzzle.

"He's even a chestnut," said Leslie, noting his color

on the few spots that were not completely covered in dirt and grime. "So he's kind of the color of a spark."

She looked over at Alex and he rolled his eyes dramatically, then smiled and winked at her to show he was teasing.

Leslie watched Dr. Burke work while she hosed Spark's legs. After examining the joint on Lucky's leg with probing fingers, the veterinarian used gauze and a cleaning gel to carefully clean the wound. Then, she applied some cream and wrapped the whole joint first in gauze and a heavy cotton wrap, then in a stretchy bandage that stuck to itself, called Vet Wrap.

When she was finished, Dr. Burke stood and pulled off her rubber gloves. "I have to be honest with you, Leslie, this hock does not look very good. I think whatever burned him hit him with some force, because there seems to be some damage to the tendons."

While she talked, she picked up her supplies and instruments and put them in the truck.

"I'm going to have to do an ultrasound to find out for sure the extent of the damage. I want to do the same thing for Fred and Spark, just to make sure there's nothing wrong with them. It's hard to tell anything for sure with all this swelling, so I'm going to wait and come back tomorrow to do it."

A heavy weight settled on Leslie's shoulders and she sighed. She had cried and worried so much that she did not feel like she could do any more, but she was starting to feel overwhelmed by the bad news.

What if Lucky's leg is permanently damaged? She thought. *His show career will be over. It's not fair!*

"You can stop hosing now," Dr. Burke continued, walking back toward them with some bottles and tubes in her hands. "Here's some Bute. It's a very good medicine, like aspirin, that reduces pain and swelling. Give each horse one gram in the morning and again at night."

She handed each item to Leslie while she explained what to do. "This is a salve for the burns. Put this on twice a day too. This one is a topical solution for pain and swelling, like the Bute. Rub it on their legs or joints if you see swelling or feel heat. This bottle is the antibiotics I mentioned to ward off any infection, and I've put the dosing instructions on the label.

"Hand walk them for ten minutes, twice per day. Fred isn't too bad, so you can ride him at the walk if you want. If there's a lot of swelling, hose it with cold water for ten minutes. Any questions?"

Alex and Leslie shook their heads solemnly. They had both helped to take care of sick or injured horses several times while working at Green Meadow, but it was hard for Leslie to see her favorite horses in pain. She thought Alex probably felt the same way, given the sad—and uncharacteristically serious—look on his face.

"Good. I'll be back around noon tomorrow to check on them. Go ahead and put them in their stalls and give them plenty to eat. They deserve it."

Dr. Burke paused and looked at them, then held out her arms to hug them. Leslie hugged back gratefully. "It'll be all right, Leslie. We'll do our best to take care of them and make them as well as we can, OK?

Leslie nodded and sniffed. "Sure thing," she said, with a smile that was braver than she felt.

Chapter Four:
Clean up

Leslie slept deeply that night. She was staying with her best friend Holly while Dan and Helen were on their honeymoon. Holly and her parents had arrived the night before, after Dr. Burke left to take Leslie home. Leslie had been so depressed and tired, despite her nap, she barely spoke on the ride to Holly's house and went straight to bed.

"I feel so bad we weren't able to get in to Green Meadow to help," Holly said at the breakfast table the next morning between bites of scrambled egg. "The road was completely cut off, and the fire department wouldn't let us in. We were so worried!"

Leslie swallowed her piece of bacon and answered. "I know you would have helped if you could have, Hol. The fire spread so fast that the fire department couldn't get in either. I don't think anyone expected it to spread like that."

Holly swallowed hard and stared at her plate, pushing her eggs around with her fork. "You must have been so scared. Julie told me about how you rode all the way to the Bakers to save their horses, then rode all the way home." She looked up at Leslie, eyes wet. "How did you do it? I don't think I could have had the courage."

Holly spoke softly and slowly, unlike her usual way where all of her words tumbled out in one breath. Leslie had known her for several years and loved her upbeat personality. She was surprised Holly was so subdued.

Leslie took a thoughtful sip of her orange juice before answering. "To tell you the truth, I don't know how I did it. I was so scared, but Alex was really brave. I just tried not to think about it, I guess.

"Knowing those horses were in danger kept me going, and then all I wanted was to get home. Lucky was amazing. I just closed my eyes and held on, and he took us all the way home. And now..."

She paused when her heart rose in her throat, and she had to swallow and fight back tears before she could continue.

"And now, he might be lame forever because of it."

The tears she was too numb to cry the night before flowed from her eyes, dripping on her plate.

Holly jumped up to wrap her arms around Leslie's shoulder in a hug. "It'll be all right, Leslie. It's not your fault; you didn't know that was going to happen. Besides, maybe he'll get better."

"I know I couldn't really have prevented it, but I can't help feeling guilty. What will I do if he can never show again?"

"Try not to think that way, Leslie. Let's just take the best care of him we can, and see what happens, OK?"

Leslie sniffed and nodded. "OK. I'll try to stay positive for Lucky. Do you think your parents are ready to take us over to Green Meadow yet?"

Holly's parents were ready, and they were soon on their way. Leslie was quiet on the ride to the barn, lost in her thoughts about Lucky. *If only we hadn't stopped to look at that horse, he probably wouldn't be hurt. I wonder how long it will take for him to be better, and if I'll ever get to show or even ride him again? I should just be thankful he's alive.*

The closer they drove to the stable, the more evidence of the fire Leslie saw. The fire had been put out in the area surrounding the stable, although Leslie could still see and smell smoke in the air.

It must still be burning somewhere, she thought. *I hope it doesn't do too much more damage.*

She gazed sadly at the ruined forest that scrolled past the window and hoped it wasn't all lost.

The car pulled into the Green Meadow parking lot a few minutes later, and Leslie was surprised and over-joyed to see Helen standing in front of the barn, talking to Julie. She had the door open almost before the car had stopped and ran the few yards to throw her arms around her trainer and new mother.

"Helen!"

Helen returned Leslie's hug fiercely, holding her tight for several minutes. Leslie clung back, happy to see her but feeling guilty all over again that her parents' honey-moon had been cut short. They had not planned to be home for several more days.

Leslie suspected Helen was as overcome with emo-tion as she was, because neither spoke or moved for a couple of minutes. Tears ran down Leslie's cheeks and her shoulders shook, and Helen held her even tighter.

"Leslie, I'm so glad you're all right. When Julie told

me what happened, I just had to come home and see everything, see you with my own eyes. You were so brave!"

"Oh, Helen. I was so scared. Alex and Lucky were my rocks. I don't know how I could have ever gotten through it without them."

Helen pulled away and held Leslie at arm's length, hands on her shoulders. She studied Leslie's face while she said softly, "First things first. I know I'll never replace your mother, but I'll do the best I can, as much as you'll let me. If you'll do me the honor of calling me Mom, it would make me happier than you could ever know. If you don't feel comfortable with that, I'll understand."

A grin spread across Leslie's face, cutting through the tears. "Oh, Mom. I'd love to!"

She liked the way it felt and sounded to call Helen that. They hugged again to seal the deal.

"Where's Dad?"

"He's right here," her father answered, walking out of the barn. Helen let go and Leslie ran to him and hugged him, breathing in his scent with a sigh of relief.

"I'm so sorry you had to cut your honeymoon short, Dad, but boy am I happy to see you!"

"I'm happy to see you too, sweetie. Don't worry, Helen and I will figure out how to make up for it some other time. Taking care of you and the ranch are more important."

He broke his hold, reached into his pocket and pulled out his car keys.

"Right now, however, I have some things to take care of. Can you two girls live without me for a few hours?" Leslie and Helen nodded. Dan waved goodbye and left.

"I wish Alex was going to be here today," Leslie said. "His mother needed him at home."

"I'm sure you do, and I can always use him around here. I guess I have to share him with his family sometimes," Helen responded with a smile. "All right, let's go see our patients. I heard those horses had a pretty rough time of it. We have a new charge to worry about?"

Leslie nodded somberly, the lightness of the previous few moments forgotten, and they walked arm in arm into the barn. It was not until then she remembered Holly and her parents. She looked over her shoulder and saw they had already driven away.

They must not have wanted to intrude, she thought. *I feel bad for getting out of the car and not saying goodbye though.*

Out loud she said, "Lucky's hurt pretty bad, Hel— Mom." She smiled briefly at her struggle over the new name, but the seriousness of the situation caused the smile to fade quickly. "He has a huge burn right on his hock, and Dr. Burke thinks there might be damage to the joint. The rest is just minor burns and scrapes, and the same for Fred. Their legs were pretty swollen from the strain too."

She stopped to get the medical supplies out of the first aid kit and some cookies from the grooming area, and then they continued toward the horses' stalls.

"And what about the horse you found?"

"Oh, Spark!" She recounted the tale of how Spark followed them home, the condition he was in and how they thought he might have been abandoned for some time.

Helen frowned. "Poor horse. Well, let's check on Lucky and Fred first, and then we can see about this Spark."

They reached Lucky's stall first and went inside. Helen gasped when she saw him. "Oh, poor Lucky. You don't look like you're feeling very well, are you?"

She gently hugged his face to her chest, then walked around him to look at his wounds.

When Helen stepped out of the way, Leslie moved in to give Lucky a hug herself. She then looked in his feeder and saw that he had not touched his breakfast.

"He didn't eat his breakfast. That's not a good sign," she said thoughtfully. "That means he definitely doesn't feel well."

She fed him some of the Bute and gave him his antibiotics while Helen put salve on his burns.

"I see his wounded hock is wrapped, so I think we should leave that for Dr. Burke. We can put the anti-inflammatory cream on his legs, though," Helen said.

Leslie attempted to feed Lucky a cookie while Helen applied the medicine, but the little gelding just lipped at it. He finally took a small bite and chewed it slowly but would not take any more.

"He usually begs for cookies," Leslie said, frowning.

Once Lucky was taken care of, they moved on to Fred's stall. He was perkier than Lucky; his eyes were brighter and his ears pricked at the sight of the cookies in Leslie's hand. She offered him one and he ate it greedily. She saw his breakfast was nearly gone.

"I guess he's feeling pretty well today, all things considered," she said, relieved.

Leslie and Helen repeated their ministrations on Fred, and then they moved on to visit Spark. Although he greeted them by pricking his ears and sniffing at them curiously, he only did this for a moment before returning to his feed bin to slowly eat his hay. His eyes were still dull, like they were the night before. Leslie offered him a cookie and he ate it.

"He's pretty emaciated and beat up. I can see why

you thought he'd been abandoned out there. Dr. Burke didn't recognize him?"

"No, but she said she would check her records and with her other clients." Leslie frowned and creased her brow. "Although... if someone set him loose on purpose, they probably won't admit it."

"You're probably right. Well, we'll do the best we can for him and take each day as it comes. If we can find his rightful owner, great. If not, we can probably make room for him here."

She chuckled and added, "I guess we're starting to look like a rescue operation, huh? First Lucky and now this guy."

Leslie smiled. "I guess I'm an unwanted horse magnet. They just keep finding me!"

Helen stood back to study their new charge.

"You know, when you look past his poor condition, the wounds and the matted hair, he's a nice horse. He has a nice face, his shoulder is at the right angle and he has a nice short back and a good hip. I think he was a nice horse before he was abandoned."

Leslie looked at Spark and recognized the nice features of him Helen had pointed out.

She nodded and replied, "I think you're right. Once we get him fattened up a little and can put him to work to put some muscle on, I bet he'll be quite handsome."

Helen's face turned serious. "Now, Leslie, don't get too attached. This horse does belong to someone, and it might not be their fault he was lost. They may want him back. We need to do everything we can to find his real owners before we get our hearts set on keeping him. We'll feed him up in the mean time, but I want you to be prepared to give him back if his owners show up, OK?"

Leslie sighed. "I know. You're right, Hel—I mean, Mom. I just wish people would take better care of their horses."

Helen smiled. "Me, too. Oh, well, we can't control what other people do. All we can do is the best we can to help the horses we can."

She led the way out of Spark's stall and Leslie followed.

"In the meantime, we have some work to do. You guys did a great job protecting the property and the buildings, but I want to ride the perimeter and just make sure there's no damage out there we need to take care of. Want to come along?"

"Sure!"

Leslie and Helen tacked up the other two lesson horses, Jade and Sarah, and rode side-by-side down the service road that would lead them to the perimeter of the ranch. Leslie looked up at the sky and could see a hint of blue through the haze of smoke.

"It would probably be a nice day if it weren't for the fire," she said.

The air was warm and close, and Leslie found it difficult to take deep breaths with the air still thick with smoke.

"We probably shouldn't push the horses too hard. This smoke can't be good for their lungs."

"I agree, and it's not good for us either. We'll just keep it to an easy walk."

"I guess all the horses will need a day or two off from work, huh?" Leslie asked.

"Yep. Even when the smoke subsides, they'll need a day or two to completely get it out of their lungs. We'll need to take the stalled horses for walks to stretch their legs, and then we'll put them back to work when the air is clear."

While they rode, they looked for signs of damage along the fence line. Leslie saw a lot of burned trees and logs, but she also saw a lot of trees and bushes that were spared.

"How can there be anything out here that isn't burned? That fire was awful!"

"I understand the fire moved very fast," Helen answered. "When fire moves that quickly, sometimes it skips over some of the fuel in its path. Although it was scary, that's a bright side."

"I guess," Leslie said sadly. "I just wish we didn't have to have fires at all."

"I know, but keep in mind: Fire is a part of nature, albeit a harsh one. It clears out the undergrowth and actually improves the fertility of the ground.

"By this time next year, the ground will be all covered with green again, lusher than ever, and new trees will be growing. We'll always have the dead trees to remind us of what happened though."

Leslie chewed over Helen's words while she rode for a few moments. "I guess that makes me feel a little better about losing all those beautiful trees, but I will be glad when it starts growing back."

"You and me both, Leslie," Helen said. Her smile was a sad one.

It took them about an hour to complete their circuit around the perimeter of the property, and they did not find any fencing that needed repair.

"We'll want to check the trails next, but we'll wait a few days until the smoke subsides," Helen said when they turned up the service road to return to the barn.

"There will be fallen trees across the trails that will need to be cleared, and it will be a lot of work. For now, I'm feeling very blessed that we didn't lose any horses or structures."

"Me too. It's really sad that the Bakers can't say the same," Leslie said, remembering the sight of the fire licking the corners of the barn while she and Alex fled.

"That's true. Unfortunately, they had a lot of dry grass around their property, and that provided fuel for the fire to spread. They lost their house too."

Leslie felt a little ill at the news. "I didn't know that. That is so sad for them."

She thought about what it would be like to lose everything she owned and added, "I can't imagine how awful that would be. I hope it never happens to me."

When they arrived at the barn, Leslie saw her father waiting for them.

"Once you get your horses undressed, come into the lounge. I brought lunch."

Leslie laughed. "It's called untacking, Dad. They aren't wearing clothes, they're wearing tack!"

Despite the six years Leslie had been around horses, with Dan taking her to her lessons and horse shows, he still did not have a full grasp of the terms or how things worked. Sometimes Leslie suspected he knew more than he let on but played dumb to make her laugh.

"Well, whatever it's called, hurry up and do it so we can eat!"

Leslie and Helen laughed, but they quickly untacked their horses and put them away. They found Dan in the lounge, which was a room that overlooked the indoor arena. It had comfortable couches, a coffee table, refrigerator and a telephone for clients to use when they wanted to relax at the barn. Helen, Julie, Leslie and Alex often ate lunch in there.

When Helen and Leslie went in, the coffee table was set with plates for each of them with turkey sandwiches on Leslie's favorite whole grain bread from the local bakery. Helen had been influencing Dan and Leslie's diet ever since she and Dan had become engaged. A serving of colorful fruit salad sat beside each sandwich, and Dan set an icy bottle of water at each of their places when Helen and Leslie sat down.

Helen sighed in appreciation as she sat. "It sure is good having you around to take care of us like this. I don't suppose you can quit your job and just be a house wife?"

Her eyes twinkled merrily when she said the last part.

Dan laughed. "That would be house *husband*, and not if you want me to keep paying bills and buying food. This one eats a surprising amount for such a little thing," he said, pointing his thumb at Leslie.

Leslie giggled. "Dad! I don't eat *that* much. Besides, I'm a growing girl. I'm not little anymore!"

"I guess I have to give you that, but you'll always be my little girl, whether you like it or not," he answered, winking at her. He gave her a soft punch on the shoulder.

While they ate, Dan and Helen told Leslie about their drive up to the Browns' cabin.

"The forest was so majestic," said Helen. "The trees were incredibly tall."

"And the road was incredibly windy," Dan put in. "I thought it was pretty fun, but Helen whined at me to slow down or she would throw up."

He smiled fondly at his new wife, who playfully slapped him on the arm.

"That's because you thought you were Dale Earn-hardt or something, you were driving so fast!"

Dan rolled his eyes in response.

They were finishing their lunch when Dr. Burke ar-rived. Dan gathered the plates and threw away the trash, shooing them out the door.

"I'll take care of this. You two go take care of the horses. I'll see you at Helen's for dinner tonight."

Helen's house was located on the property, just a short walk from the barn. Leslie had not been surprised when her father told her he would be putting their house on the market to sell so they could move into Helen's, but she had been very happy she would be living so close to the horses. They still had to move all of their stuff over from the old house to the new one, a task that had been scheduled for after the honeymoon was over.

Helen walked out to meet Dr. Burke while Leslie went to Lucky's stall to bring him out. He did not seem to have moved since she had left that morning, although more of his breakfast was gone.

At least he's not completely off his feed, she thought, *but I wish he were eating better.*

She slipped his halter over his nose and buckled it behind his ears, and then spoke soothing words to him and stroked him until Dr. Burke and Helen arrived at the stall. Dr. Burke stepped into the stall and knelt by Lucky's back leg. Using a pair of scissors that were flat on one side, she cut the bandage off that covered his wound. When she saw the ruined flesh, Leslie felt a wave of nau-sea and swayed on her feet. Immediately, Helen was be-side her with an arm around her shoulders, steadying her.

Dr. Burke set up a machine she had brought with her next to Lucky. She gently slathered some gel from a tube all over the joint, and then delicately went over it with a wand that was attached to the machine with a cord, watching the small screen on the machine with a frown. Lucky flinched several times, and Leslie blew softly into his nose, trying to convey how she loved him, hoping it would soothe him.

The veterinarian worked quietly for a few minutes, examining the same area on both hocks for comparison, then sighed and put the wand away.

"I have to be honest with you, Leslie. This leg does not look good. The burn will heal with time and medication, but I'm really concerned about the damage to the tendons that tie in here to the joint. It looks like whatever hit him hit pretty hard."

Helen squeezed Leslie's shoulders a little tighter, and Leslie leaned heavily against her. Leslie swallowed hard and asked, "Is-is there anything you can do for him? Will he always be lame?"

"I really can't tell you for sure. The best we can do is keep it wrapped, put him on stall rest with a little hand walking every day and recheck him after a couple of weeks. We'll keep him on the Bute, which will help. We just need to take it day by day. Sometimes horses come back from something like this eventually with no problem, and others are never right again."

Leslie gasped, one hand covering her mouth and the other wrapping around her suddenly aching stomach. Dr. Burke's face softened and Leslie could see the regret in her eyes.

"I'm sorry I can't give you better news. I know how much he means to you."

She stood, wiped her hands on her jeans, and then put them on Leslie's shoulders. She looked earnestly into

Leslie's eyes and added, "I promise, I'll do the very best I can for him. For now, he needs you to be strong, OK?"

Leslie nodded, swiping at the tears and taking a deep, shuddering breath to try to bring them under control. "You're right. My being upset will only upset him."

She wished she could believe it was that easy to be brave for Lucky.

"That's right. Keep positive."

"Let's be thankful, Leslie," Helen put in. "This could have been much worse. You and Lucky could have died, but he got you home safely. If worse comes to worst, he can live the good life in the pasture and you can visit him every day."

Leslie managed a small smile at that.

"Yes, and if we're really lucky, maybe you'll be able to ride him again," Dr. Burke added.

Leslie had her tears under control, and she lifted her head and squared her shoulders.

"OK. I'm prepared for the worst but hopeful for the best. If I can never show him again, I at least have my memories from this year."

It was hard for her to say it, but she knew it was true.

No sense in dwelling on it, she thought. *What will be, will be. At least he's alive.*

"Very mature of you, Leslie," Dr. Burke said with an approving nod. "Now, how about we check on the other two patients?"

Leslie removed Lucky's halter and buckled it onto the bar on his stall door before giving him a kiss on the nose and closing the door behind her. Dr. Burke had already started her examination of Fred when Leslie arrived at his stall, and the veterinarian had a pleased smile on her face.

"He's looking pretty good, considering what he went

through. Give him a few days off, but then he'll be fine to go back to work. His legs are still a little swollen, so go ahead and hose them with cold water again, and keep hand walking him for ten minutes twice a day. Keep up with the Bute and anti-inflammatory cream, but he can go out in a paddock or pasture to stretch his legs."

Helen smiled and put her arm around Leslie's shoulders and squeezed.

"At least we have some good news!"

Leslie added her half-hearted smile in agreement. She was happy to learn that Fred would be good as new soon, particularly after the bad news about Lucky.

The three stepped out of Fred's stall and walked to Spark's together.

"Like Fred, Spark's wounds are pretty minor, so he should get over them pretty soon. Keep treating him just like Fred. A little cold hosing, hand walking and turn-out, and he'll be just fine. Your biggest task is to get him fattened up. Are you giving him bran mashes?"

Leslie nodded. "We're also giving him rice bran and beet pulp."

Dr. Burke nodded her approval. "Good job. Just be patient, and that weight will be on in no time."

Leslie, Helen and Dr. Burke started walking toward the barn entrance, the veterinarian carrying the ultrasound machine. "I haven't had much chance to ask around among my clients, but I'll let you know if I find anything out," she said. "In any case, I'll be back the day after tomorrow to check on everyone."

"Thank you so much for everything, Dr. Burke. I'm sure you have a lot of work on your hands with the fire," Helen said.

"I sure do. Unfortunately, there were a lot of injuries,

and some horses got sick from smoke inhalation."

Leslie and Helen walked Dr. Burke to her truck and helped her load her things in, then waved as she drove away. No sooner had she driven out the gate than another car pulled in, one Leslie did not recognize.

"Do you know who that is, Mom?"

Inwardly, she thought, *I guess I'm already getting used to calling her that. I like it.* The thought made her smile.

Helen did not seem to notice, because she was staring at the car. "I don't recognize the car. Let's wait here to see who it is."

They backed up to leave room for the car to park. When the middle-aged coupled stepped out, Leslie recognized their faces.

"Mr. and Mrs. Baker!" she exclaimed in surprise.

"Hello, Leslie, Helen," Mr. Baker said, walking around the car to stand beside his wife. His eyes were drawn and his face looked haggard. Leslie did not blame him, considering what they had been through.

"We wanted to stop by and thank Leslie and Alex for what they did yesterday. That was very heroic of you, Leslie."

"That's so nice!" Helen said. "Alex isn't here, unfortunately. I'm sure he would have loved to see that you are all right."

"That's too bad. I hope you'll tell him we came by."

"Those horses mean everything to us," Mrs. Baker added. "We've lost our barn, our house, everything but the horses and the fences. We can replace the things, but we could never replace our beloved horses. When we couldn't get in to our property to get them, we thought for sure they would be lost. The thought of them suffering—" She broke off and put a hand to her mouth, and it was a moment before she was able to continue.

Leslie's heart ached for her.

"We couldn't believe it when the fire passed and we went in to find them in the arena, safe and sound. Of course, they weren't very happy about having to stand under the sprinklers all that time!" She managed to chuckle a little at that, but her eyes were as sad as her husband's.

"You're welcome. I can't imagine leaving them, knowing they were in the barn and the fire was so close. Alex and I just did what we knew we had to do," Leslie said, blushing and looking at her feet. She felt Helen reach over and squeeze her hand.

"Well, it was very brave of you. Dr. Burke told us it was you who saved them, and that your horses were injured in the fire. We feel so badly about that," Mr. Baker said.

"Well, thank you, but I didn't feel brave. I was scared out of my mind! I'm sure the horses will be all right, though. They need some rest, but I'm sure they'll be good as new soon," Leslie said. *I wish that were true about Lucky,* she thought, *but I don't want them to feel bad about that. It's not their fault.*

"You know, Leslie, bravery is not about not being scared," Mrs. Baker said with a smile. "Bravery is about doing what needs to be done, even when you're afraid."

Leslie smiled at that, feeling her chest swell with pride. She squeezed Helen's hand, but couldn't bring herself to look at anyone.

"You and Alex were heroes, Leslie," Mr. Baker said. "I wish we could give you something to show our appreciation, but as we said, we lost everything." His voice broke a little at the end, and Leslie's heart ached again.

"Thank you, but just the fact the horses are OK is enough. I'm glad you two were safe too," Leslie said, fighting her bashfulness to look him in the eye.

She didn't know why she felt so embarrassed; she was normally outgoing and talkative. However, she was not used to the feeling of being a hero and did not know how to react.

Mrs. Baker stepped closer to Leslie and held her arms out for a hug, and Leslie gladly obliged, letting go of Helen's hand.

"We just wanted to come over and thank you in person," the older woman said, then released her hold.

"Will you two be OK?" Helen asked. "Where will you go? Will you rebuild?"

"Our daughter and her husband have a place in town, so we're staying with them," Mr. Baker answered. "Thankfully, our pastures are intact, so we can keep the horses on our property. We will definitely rebuild. Thank God for our homeowner's insurance!"

The Bakers bid their goodbyes, climbed into their car and drove away. Watching their car disappear down the road, Helen said, "What a marvelous, positive outlook they have. Here they've lost nearly everything they own, and yet they don't complain. They're already talking about rebuilding and going on with their lives. That's a good lesson for anyone, Leslie."

Leslie nodded, smiling. "You're right. There's no sense in lamenting the bad things that happen to you. That doesn't solve anything, does it?"

"It sure doesn't. Now, come on. We have some horses to take care of." Helen put her arm around Leslie's shoulder and led her into the barn.

At five o'clock, Helen and Leslie left the barn and walked to the house. Dan was in the kitchen, wearing an apron and cooking something Leslie thought smelled spicy and delicious.

"Mmm smells good!" Leslie said. "Tacos?"

"You got it. My favorite girl's favorite food!" he answered with a wink. The table was loaded with bowls of lettuce, shredded cheese, diced tomatoes, olives, and sour cream. Dan motioned for Helen and Leslie to sit while he placed a steaming bowl of seasoned meat in front of them. He pulled a plate full of pan-fried corn tortillas out of the oven.

"All right, ladies, dig in!"

All three happily did so, and for a few minutes the only conversation at the table was that of requests to pass this or that while they ate. Once the eating slowed, Dan asked, "So how was your day?"

Leslie told him about Dr. Burke's visit and Lucky's uncertain future. She tried to be brave and stay positive, but the tears piled up in her eyes and nearly escaped. She took a deep breath and refused to allow herself to cry, but it was hard to get the words out to tell the whole story.

Helen looked at her and smiled, squeezing her knee under the table. If she hadn't been so hungry, and if tacos weren't her favorite food, she would have lost her appetite just thinking about poor Lucky.

"I'm really sorry to hear that, Les," Dan said, concern evident in his eyes. "I'll keep thinking positive for him. I'm sure he'll be OK."

"Thanks, Dad."

"We had some visitors this afternoon," Helen said,

changing the subject. "The Bakers stopped by to thank Alex and Leslie for saving their horses. They said the kids were heroes."

Leslie blushed. She looked at her plate. "They said they lost everything in the fire but their fences and their horses. They have to start all over again."

"I can't imagine going through that," Dan said somberly. "When we heard about the fire, we headed straight back here. We were really worried, but so relieved when we pulled in and everything was still here."

"Julie was great," Leslie said. "She had everyone working, spraying down the buildings, sending Juan and Josh out to fight the fire with the big hoses. Everyone who was there pitched in and helped."

They had all finished eating, so they worked together to clear the table and load the dishwasher. Once they were done, Dan announced, "Well, as you know, I've been busy all day. I think it's time I show you what I've been up to."

He looked at Helen and winked, and she winked back. Leslie had the distinct impression they were up to something.

Dan led the way up the stairs. Leslie followed, puzzled.

"What are you so secretive about?" she asked

"You'll see," was the only answer she received.

The three walked down the hall, and Dan stopped them at the door to the guest room, where Leslie sometimes stayed when he was out of town for work. He had a big smile on his face, further adding to Leslie's suspicion that he had something planned.

"I redecorated a little. Why don't you go in and see if you approve of my work?" he said.

Leslie had never known her father to be a decorator. Most of the décor in their home had been put there by her mother, and he had never changed anything. She opened the door, turned on the light, and froze in surprise.

It was her room. The room she had grown up in, for as long as she could remember, only in Helen's house. Every piece of furniture, every picture, every knick knack was set up in the guest room in the exact same way as it had been at their old house.

"Dad! This is amazing! You did all this by yourself?" She was still too surprised to move.

"Yep. Took me all day, but I did it. Helen and I talked it over on the drive home, and decided you and I might as well move in tonight. I trust that's OK with you?"

Leslie recovered enough from the pleasant surprise to remember how to make her muscles work. She turned around and threw her arms around him. "OK? I love it!"

Chapter Five:
Moving Day

When Leslie woke up the next morning, she almost didn't remember she was in her new home. It was not until she opened the door to go to the bathroom and saw the hallway with everything in the wrong place and the wrong art on the walls that she remembered where she was. When she did, she hugged herself and smiled.

"Welcome home!" she said softly to herself.

The scent of coffee floated up the stairs and tickled her nostrils. She couldn't stand the stuff, but it was a smell she loved because it told her that her father was up and cooking breakfast.

She hurried down the hall to the bathroom, then downstairs to see what was for breakfast. Her parents bustled around the kitchen together; Dan poured the coffee and Helen flipped pancakes. There was a glass of orange juice on the table at Leslie's place.

"Good morning!" she said. She sat and took a sip of her juice.

"Good morning!" Dan and Helen said at the same time. Everyone laughed.

"How did you sleep?" Helen asked. She placed a plate stacked high with pancakes in the middle of the table.

"Great. I almost forgot I was here until I came out of my room this morning!" Leslie said, laughing.

She used a fork to put two pancakes on each of their plates while Dan placed coffee and cream on the table. Helen added butter and syrup.

"When will we move the rest of our stuff, Dad?"

"Well, I have a few more days off work, so I'll work on it. Maybe you can help me a little this morning before you come back and work with Helen?"

"Is that OK, Mom?" She realized her new name for Helen rolled off her tongue much more easily than it had the day before.

"Sure. In fact, there really isn't that much for you to do, since none of the horses are being exercised for another day or two. Why don't you take all morning to help your dad, then we can have lunch and you can help me after that? I'll take care of our patients this morning and you can do it later."

"Sounds good."

It was Monday and an in service day, so Leslie did not have school. She did not look forward to going back the next day. High school had started two weeks before, and while she enjoyed it, she would much rather be home with her parents and the horses.

After breakfast, Leslie dressed and climbed into Helen's truck with her father, and they drove to their old house.

While he drove, Dan asked, "So, how do you feel about moving, Leslie? You've lived in this house your whole life."

He watched the road but glanced at her out of the corner of his eye when he asked.

Leslie thought about her feelings for a moment before she answered. "I have mixed feelings. On the one hand, there are a lot of memories at our old house. It's where I knew Mom."

Saying that made Leslie feel a little guilty. "My real Mom."

She felt badly about that, too. "Well, you know..."

"It's OK, Leslie. Your real mother was very special, and always will be, but it's OK to love Helen and call her Mom too. Claire would have wanted it this way," Dan said gently.

Leslie looked down at her hands. "Yeah, I'm sure you're right. It just sounds funny sometimes, you know?"

"I understand." He looked at her with concern in his eyes for a moment before returning his attention to the road.

Leslie studied her hands intently. "Anyway, it's hard to pack up and move away from it, like I'm moving away from Mom. But on the other hand, I'm looking forward to our new life with my new Mom and living with the horses.

"It's like we're starting off on a grand adventure, but it's our new life. Does that sound silly?" She snuck a look at him out of the corner of his eye to gauge his reaction.

"Not at all," he said. He smiled to reassure her.

They pulled into the driveway of their old house a few minutes later. Dan had piled some empty boxes in the bed of the truck, and they spent a few minutes unloading them and carrying them in the house.

"Since Helen's house is completely furnished, we're going to put all of our household stuff in storage," Dan said. "She has that big shed in the back that has almost nothing in it, so we'll put it all in there and cover everything with tarps."

"Dad, do you think we could move *some* of our things into the house?"

"Well, it's really not necessary, because she has everything we need. It would just get crowded, honey. Now come on, let's get to work. I'll pack up the kitchen, and why don't you start in the bathrooms?"

Leslie grabbed a box and stomped down the hall to the downstairs bathroom. She snatched things out of the cupboards and tossed them in the box.

"How can he just put all of our old things, everything Mom picked out, in storage?" she angrily asked the bathroom sink.

She was surprised at how angry she felt. She loved Helen and was happy to live at Green Meadow, her favorite place in the world, but she felt as though she was betraying her mother to be packing everything away and forgetting about it, like their life with her mother didn't even exist.

"How can Dad do this to Mom? Doesn't he miss her at all?"

Leslie couldn't bear to look at or talk to her father all morning. She avoided him, moving from room to room and packing, fuming over his decision.

"He didn't even consult me to see if this was what I wanted!" She complained to the books she pulled off a shelf in the living room and dropped them into a box.

Dan walked in. "What's all the noise in here? Hey, be gentle with those books, OK?"

"Sorry," Leslie mumbled, crouching down to straighten them in the box. She refused to look at him.

"Is there something wrong, Les?"

"I don't want to talk about it!" she snapped back and turned away so he would not see the tears stinging her eyes.

If he doesn't know what he's done wrong, I'm certainly not going to tell him! she thought.

She busied herself pulling books off the shelf and piling them in her arms until she heard his footsteps retreat down the hall. She angrily put them in the box and wiped her eyes, then went back to her work of packing.

By the time much of the house was packed and the truck was loaded to capacity, it was nearly time for lunch.

"Let's head on over to the new house now," Dan said. "I'll make us some sandwiches, and then you can help me unload the big stuff before you go out to the barn, OK?"

"Whatever," Leslie muttered, climbing into the cab of the truck and buckling her seatbelt. She stared out the window, refusing to look at her father. He must have noticed she was not in the mood to talk, because he remained silent on the ride to Green Meadow.

It was not until they pulled up to the house that he spoke again. "So, what kind of sandwich would you like? I have salami, turkey, ham..." his voice trailed off, and Leslie could see out of the corner of her eye that he was looking at her.

The thought of eating anything made her stomach clench. "I don't want anything. I'm not hungry."

All she wanted to do was cry, but she did not want to do it in front of him, because he would want her to tell him what was wrong. She wasn't ready to talk about it yet. She jumped out of the truck, slammed the door, and ran into the barn to Lucky's stall. She let herself inside, closed the stall door behind her and collapsed in the freshly cleaned shavings before bursting into tears.

She buried her face in her hands. She then felt her horse's warm breath on her fingers. He sniffed her softly, which made her cry all the harder. She didn't know why, but Lucky's gentle nudges made her miss her mother more than ever. Through her tears, she heard him step closer. He pushed more insistently at her hands, running his muzzle up and down each arm. Finally, she relented and took her hands off her face. She nearly jumped at seeing Lucky's face so close to hers, even though she had known he was there. That made her laugh a little, and she wrapped her arms around his head and hugged him close.

"Oh, Lucky," she said. She sniffed. "Here you are, hurting, but you're comforting me when I'm sad. You're a good friend."

Lucky let out a big sneeze and sprayed her with horse snot.

"Yuck!" she said, wiping off her face before scratching him affectionately behind the ears.

She didn't know how long she sat like that, holding his head in her arms, but they both jumped a little when the door slid slowly open and Helen's face appeared in the doorway. She did know that she felt better than when she had entered the stall.

"Leslie?" Leslie turned her face away and didn't respond. "Leslie, your father told me you were upset, but he wasn't sure why."

Leslie heard the rustle of shavings when her stepmother stepped closer and knelt down beside her, but still she said nothing. Helen placed her hand on Leslie's shoulder.

"Sweetie, won't you talk to me? If you tell me what's

wrong, maybe I can help you fix it."

Leslie took a deep, shuddering breath and let it out, eyes trained on her horse so she wouldn't have to look Helen in the eye. She barely knew what was wrong, let alone how to explain so Helen would understand. She opened her mouth to speak, then shut it and shook her head.

"Was it something to do with moving?" Helen asked. "Are you sad to be moving out of your old house? I know you grew up there, so it must be hard for you to leave it behind."

"It's not just that," Leslie said, still unsure of exactly what she wanted to say. "It's—I don't know. You wouldn't understand."

She picked up a shaving from the stall floor and picked it apart with her fingers.

Helen shifted and sat down Indian-style, facing Leslie. She put her hand on Leslie's knee and looked intently at her.

"Try me, Leslie. We've been friends for a long time, and I think I know you better than just about anyone. It's not often I see you like this. You've never held secrets from me before."

Leslie took another deep breath and tried again, still looking anywhere but at Helen.

"You know I love you, and I'm really excited to live at Green Meadow, but it's just not fair," she burst out. She wasn't sure that was the right way to begin, and she bit her lip in consternation.

"What's not fair, Leslie?" Helen asked gently, softly squeezing Leslie's knee.

Leslie searched for the right words again. "It's like— well—" she couldn't believe how hard it was to express her feelings. "It's like we're just forgetting Mom ever existed. Like we're taking all of her memories of her and throwing them away. It's not fair. What would she think, if she's looking down at us from Heaven right now, and seeing us put all her stuff in storage?"

"Is this about you calling me Mom? Because if it is, you don't have to call me that. You can go back to calling me Helen; I won't mind. I don't want you to feel uncomfortable."

Leslie bit her lip again. She had to find a way to make Helen understand. "No, no, it's not that. It's that we're taking all of the things from our house, all the things Mom and Dad and I picked out and filled our house with, and putting them in storage—in a dusty old shed. It's like Dad's trying to forget she ever existed."

Despite her effort to stop them, tears spilled out of her eyes again and she buried her face in her hands, letting them flow freely now that they were out.

"Oh, Leslie. I'm so sorry," Helen said softly. She wrapped her arms around Leslie and pulled her close. "The very last thing I would ever want would be to make it seem like we're trying to forget Claire. She was a wonderful wife and mother, and I liked her very much. Sometimes I feel a little guilty for marrying your father. I've lain awake some nights, thinking about it long and hard, wondering if I was doing the right thing or if I was betraying Claire. I talked it over with your father too.

"Finally, we decided that it's been a long time since her death, and she would want him to be happy."

She released her hold on Leslie and took her hands in her own. "Did you know he has a framed portrait from their wedding on his nightstand here?"

Leslie looked directly at Helen for the first time that

afternoon and shook her head. "It's right next to a portrait from our wedding. He asked me if I minded and I told him I didn't, that I would love to have it there. He hasn't forgotten her, Leslie. I just don't think he thought about what it would mean to you to put everything in storage."

Leslie looked down at their hands. "I'm sure you're right, but can't we have just a few things in your house to remind us of her? I love some of those things."

Helen took Leslie's chin in her fingers and turned Leslie's head so she could look her in the eye. "Leslie, we can put whatever you like in the house. It's not my house anymore; it's all of ours. And if you want to bring in some of the things that are special to you, we'll make room, or even swap some things out and put mine in storage. OK?"

Leslie sniffed and nodded. "I would really like that. Thanks…Mom."

She opened her arms for a hug, and the two clung to each other for a few moments.

When they let go, Helen smiled and said, "Now that we have that all straightened out, can we go in and have lunch? I'm starving, and your father's worried about you. We need to go in and tell him he needs to change his storage plans."

Leslie smiled back. "Now that you mention it, I am a little hungry."

"Good. Now, help me up. Women my age aren't meant to sit on the ground!"

Leslie laughed. She jumped up and reached down to help Helen stand. They walked arm-in-arm to the house, where Dan was setting the table with sandwiches and glasses of ice water. He looked up when they walked into the room, and the look of relief on his face when he saw Leslie was no longer mad at him was obvious.

"Well, hello, you two. Ready for lunch?" Leslie guessed he was going to forget about the incident earlier in the day, but she did not feel right about letting it go without an explanation and an apology.

"First, Dad, I want to tell you I'm sorry I got so mad. I was just upset because you wanted to put all of Mom's things in storage. I felt like you wanted to turn your back on Mom and everything we knew and did with her."

Dan froze, and his face fell. "Oh, Leslie. I am so sorry. I never thought of it that way, and it never occurred to me that it would affect you like that."

He held out his arms and she gladly stepped into them, hugging him tightly.

"If I knew, I would never have insisted on putting all of our old things in storage. Why didn't you say something?"

"I'm sorry, Dad; I don't know why I didn't. I just figured if you didn't know, you didn't care, and I felt like I shouldn't have to tell you. But Mom told me you can't read minds and I should just tell you how I feel."

Leslie could not help smiling while she spoke.

"Yes, men are notoriously bad mind readers," he said, squeezing her tightly. "But now that I know, we can find room in the house for some of our favorite things, can't we, Helen? Do you mind?"

"Not at all," Helen said. "In fact, I was going to insist on it if you didn't offer!"

"Well, now that that's settled, what do you say we eat lunch? Our sandwiches are getting cold."

Leslie looked at the table. "Dad!" she said, laughing. "They're egg salad. They're supposed to be cold!"

"Oh, that's right. Well, how about we eat because I'm hungry?"

They sat to eat, talking about what pieces of furniture from the old house they would like to move into Helen's and where they could put it. After they ate, Helen and Leslie helped Dan unload the truck and then went to the barn to work while he worked on the moving tasks.

"Let's take all of the horses for walks in the indoor arena to let them stretch their legs," Helen suggested. "That will keep them from getting too stir crazy, sitting in their stalls all the time."

"Sounds good. Is Alex here?"

"Yep. Maybe you two can do the walking while I catch up on paperwork in the office?"

"That would be great."

She found Alex in the tack room cleaning a bridle. "Want to help me hand walk the horses?" she asked.

He agreed, and they walked together down the barn aisle to the first two stalls. They each haltered a horse and led them to the indoor arena.

"How long do we walk them for?" Alex asked.

"Just about ten minutes or so. Just enough to let them feel like they're getting out of their stalls for a little while and get their blood pumping a little," Leslie explained while they walked. "The air quality is too bad to let them run around or do anything that would get them breathing heavy. It's very bad for their lungs, just like it is for us."

"Boy, I'm getting my exercise too," Alex said. "Jade's apparently happy to get out!"

Leslie laughed. The horse Alex led pulled him along, and he had to constantly snap the lead rope to tell her to slow down.

"Are you taking her for a walk, or is she taking you for one?" she teased.

"Very funny!"

They made their way down the barn aisle, walking each of the horses until all of them had had a chance to get out for some exercise. When they were done, it was still mid-afternoon and there was nothing left to do.

"I guess we could clean tack," Leslie said.

"I already did most of it," Alex replied, "but there are a couple of things left."

"I have a better idea," Helen put in, walking up to them. "Why don't we go to town for some ice cream? I'll get Dan to drive us and we can have a double date. If you don't mind having a couple of old farts along to buy the ice cream, that is."

Leslie grinned. "Any old fart who buys me ice cream is welcome in my book. Sounds fun! What do you say, Alex?"

"I'd love to! May I use the office phone to call my mom and ask her?"

"Sure, and tell her we'll drop you off at home afterward."

Both Alex's mother and Dan said yes, and the two couples climbed into the car to drive into town.

"What a good idea," Dan said while he drove. "It's so muggy and hot out with the fire, and I've been sweaty all day with moving. Ice cream was a great idea."

Leslie had to agree. Her hair was soaked with sweat and her skin felt salty and damp.

I think I'll take a cold shower when I get home, she thought. *Anything to get this grime off me.*

The ice cream parlor was packed with customers trying to escape the heat, and the four of them had to wait about ten minutes before they could get a table. They sipped ice water while poring over the brightly illustrated menus.

"Anyone know what they're going to get?" Helen asked.

"I'm trying to decide between the jersey, which has vanilla ice cream and chocolate whipped cream, and a caramel sundae," Leslie replied. "I love their caramel sauce here. It's so rich and sticky."

"Those both sound good," Alex said, "but I love the hot fudge. I'm getting a sundae with plenty of nuts and whipped cream and a cherry."

"I think I'll go with an ice cream soda," Dan said.

The harried-looking waiter arrived and took their orders, then hurried away as quickly as he had come.

"I guess we're not the only ones to have this idea," Helen said with a chuckle.

Dan winked. "Yeah, who knew ice cream would be so popular when it's this hot out?"

Helen punched him lightly on the arm and said, "Quiet, you. I've seen the size of those ice cream sodas they have here. You thought it was a pretty good idea yourself!"

"I can't disagree with that."

Their ice cream arrived a short time later, and the four of them set to eating. They were too busy spooning ice cream in their mouths to talk for a while, but Leslie just enjoyed the company and the rich ice cream the parlor was famous for. After the events of the previous days, the simple, normal act of the four of them going out for ice cream was a welcome change.

Chapter Six:
Spark

As the days passed, the invalid horses steadily improved. After a week, Lucky was still confined to his stall except for his daily walks, but Fred and Spark were allowed to spend time in the paddocks to stretch their legs and enjoy the sunshine. The fires had been put out and the air was clearing, and it was becoming much more pleasant to be outside. Best of all, as far as Leslie was concerned, the horses were back to work.

One day, Leslie led Spark out to the paddock and he nuzzled her arm.

"You're kind of sweet, aren't you, boy?" Leslie said affectionately, patting him on the neck.

He snorted and tossed his head, then arched his neck and pranced beside her. Leslie laughed. "I guess you're feeling better now that you're being taken care of, eh? I don't think I've seen this much life in you before!"

When they reached the paddock gate, she unlatched it and led him inside, latched the gate and removed his halter. Spark leapt away, bucking and kicking. He ran and pranced around the enclosure while Leslie watched and laughed. He stopped to blow from time to time to show his good spirits. Leslie whooped and ran after him, encouraging him to run and play. He pranced away from her with his tail over his back, lifting his knees and hocks high.

"He sure looks like he's feeling better."

Leslie jumped and turned around to see Alex sitting on the fence and grinning at her. She had been so preoccupied with playing with Spark that she had not noticed him there. A smile split her face, and she ran over to him. He jumped off the fence and wrapped his arms around her, and they just stood there for a moment, enjoying their embrace.

"Alex, I'm so glad you're here. I've hardly seen you all week; we've both been so busy," she said into his shoulder.

"You're telling me! I've missed you like crazy, but between helping my mom and your moving, we just keep missing each other."

Leslie could feel him sniffing her hair while he spoke, and she realized he had grown in the few months they had been together.

"But Mom doesn't need me anymore for a while, so I can be here every day again."

He pulled back slightly and planted a kiss on her lips.

"I've wanted to do that all week," he said, and she could hear the smile in his voice.

She pulled back so she could look him in the face. "You're not the only one!"

"Well, now that we have that out of the way, I guess we can get to the important things, like checking out the new horse," he said playfully, winking at her.

She released her hold on him and socked him on the

shoulder. "At least you know your place in the barn, Alex. That's why we keep you around."

They laughed and turned to watch Spark, who had stopped his antics a few feet away to stare at them curiously. He perked his ears at them and reached his nose out to sniff at them.

Leslie laughed. "What's the matter, Spark? Never seen two humans hug and kiss before?"

Spark responded by snorting and trotting away.

"I wonder if he's broke to ride?" Alex mused.

"Me too. He's a really nice horse. He could even be a show horse, if he's registered. I wonder who owns him."

"Yeah, me too. He definitely looks like an Arabian, maybe even a purebred. Has Dr. Burke found any leads yet?"

"Nope, not yet, and she's checked her records and asked all her clients. I guess we'll just keep feeding him and taking care of him until someone shows up. If no one ever does, I suppose we'll keep him."

"I just can't get over the fact that someone would abandon him in the woods like that. It's just not right." Alex frowned.

"I'm with you, but what can we do? If he belongs to someone, they have the right to explain themselves and maybe get him back. If we're lucky, we'll find the owner and either they'll be glad to see him and promise to take better care of him, or they'll sign over his papers to us. Nothing to do but wait and see, I guess," Leslie shrugged.

"Well, shall we leave Spark to have some alone time while we get started on stalls?"

"I thought you'd never ask, you romantic, you!" Leslie laughed and they turned to walk arm-in-arm toward the barn.

Alex and Leslie both cleaned stalls and helped to exercise horses to pay for their lessons with Helen. Alex had only been working at the barn for a few months, so his duties were limited to simple tasks, while Leslie was responsible for working some of the horses that came in for training, under Helen's supervision.

They usually split the stall cleaning duties, with Leslie doing a few and Alex doing the rest. That day, they worked together so they could enjoy each other's company while they worked. Before long, Leslie's share was finished, and she left Alex to finish while she worked horses.

Outside of the barn office hung a pen board with each horse's name, what was to be done with it that day, and who was to do it. Although Helen was the head trainer, she delegated a lot of the training work to Julie and Leslie. Helen oversaw the training schedule and observed to make sure the horses were trained to her satisfaction so the clients would be happy with the end result.

Leslie looked at the pen board and saw that she was assigned to work two horses. She was to longe one and ride the other, which made her happy. She did not get to ride every day, but she jumped at the opportunity every chance she could. Although not all of the tasks she was assigned at the barn were pleasant, they were a trade-off for the jobs she really loved to do.

And no matter what I do here, she thought, *at least I'm working with horses!*

Two more weeks passed, and still there was no word of Spark's owner. Fred was back to his job as the trusty lesson horse, but Lucky was not doing much better. Dr. Burke visited one morning to check on his progress. Helen was in the outdoor arena teaching lessons, so Leslie met with the veterinarian alone.

After using the ultrasound machine on Lucky's hock, Dr. Burke sighed and stood up. "I'm sorry to say that his progress is much slower that I had hoped, Leslie."

She frowned, and Leslie's stomach turned over. She had been hoping to hear better news.

"He is a little better, but there's still a lot of healing to do."

"Do you think he'll ever get better?" Leslie's voice sounded strained to her own ears, and she struggled to bring it under control.

"There's just no way to tell, Leslie. I'm sorry. You can take him for longer walks now, and take him outside to get some fresh air and grass, but try to keep him quiet."

Leslie nodded. *At least I can take him for walks. That's something,* she thought. She sighed and tried to smile.

"Thank you for everything, Dr. Burke. You've really been great."

Dr. Burke reached out and gave Leslie a hug.

"Chin up, Leslie. We're doing all we can for him, and I know you're doing your best. He looks like he feels better."

She let go with her left arm and turned to look at Lucky with her right arm still around Leslie's shoulders.

"See how much brighter his eyes are? And didn't you say he's eating better?"

Leslie had to agree with her; Lucky did look much happier.

"You're right. He must be feeling better. I'm sure he'll be happy to get out a little. I just wish his leg would heal faster!"

"In the meantime, let's go check on Spark. I haven't

seen him in a while, and I want to see how he's coming along."

She pulled the ultrasound machine out of Lucky's stall, and they closed the door behind them before walking down the aisle together to Spark's stall.

Dr. Burke let out a low whistle when she saw him.

"Wow. Now that you've gotten some weight on him and he's getting some exercise, he's become quite a looker! Even his coat is looking better. Great job, Leslie!"

Leslie forgot her worries over Lucky for the moment while she basked in the veterinarian's praise.

"Thank you! He's really a doll to work with. I've been grooming him and taking him out to the paddock every day. I started longeing him on a line this week, and he's responding really well. And you should see him move! He's got some great action."

She smiled and her cheeks flushed with pleasure at the thought of the chestnut's progress.

"Now that he's fattened up a little and looking more like himself, maybe you should make a flyer with a picture to post at the feed and tack stores. Maybe someone will recognize him," Dr. Burke suggested.

Leslie frowned.

"I guess I could do that." She could not seem to look the veterinarian in the eye when she answered.

"Leslie, you know he must have an owner somewhere. It's only right to try to find them. Don't you think?"

"I suppose. But, if his real owner turned him loose on purpose, how can I send him back to a home that won't take care of him?"

"You don't know that, Leslie. Now, I can't force you to do anything, but I hope you'll make the decision to do the right thing."

Dr. Burke looked at her intently, and Leslie nodded in agreement.

"OK, I need to get going on the rest of my rounds. Keep up the good work, Leslie. You're doing a great job."

Leslie smiled in thanks and waved while she watched the older woman leave.

"I guess I have to do the right thing, but I don't have to like it," she told herself. She walked toward Lucky's stall. Opening the door, she said to him, "I bet you're anxious to get out of there, aren't you, sweet boy? Let's go for your walk."

Lucky snorted and bobbed his head up and down, almost like he was answering her. She laughed and unbuckled his halter from the door.

"Does Lucky get to have some exercise now?" Holly's voice sounded from over Leslie's shoulder.

Leslie turned around and managed a brave smile. "Just for walks, still, but he can go outside as long as I keep him quiet. I guess it's better than nothing, but Dr. Burke wasn't very happy with his progress. She doesn't seem to think he's healing fast enough."

Her eyes started to fill with tears again, but she swallowed and willed them away unsuccessfully.

Holly quickly flashed a big smile. "Come on, Les. Let's give Lucky his walk together. I'll go with you to keep you company! Isn't it nice that he gets to go outside? I bet he'll be happy, aren't you boy?" She directed the last over Leslie's shoulder to Lucky.

Leslie giggled; Holly had a habit of running her sentences together and speaking so quickly that she said a lot in one breath. Somehow, she always managed to make Leslie smile.

"Thanks, Hol. I'd love the company. Alex is cleaning stalls, so I guess you'll have to do." She smiled to show she was joking, and Holly winked back.

Leslie slipped Lucky's halter on over his nose and led him slowly out of his stall. He perked up when he realized he was going out and followed her eagerly.

"Now, Lucky, don't get too excited," she told him mock sternly. "You have to take it easy with that leg!"

Although he was obviously happy to have the chance to get some fresh air, Lucky was still limping and he slowed his pace almost immediately. Leslie and Holly walked along on either side of him, allowing him to choose his own speed. By the time they went outside and got as far as the paddocks, Leslie decided he'd had enough and turned back to put him away.

While they walked, Leslie caught Holly up on what was going on with Spark, although she left out Dr. Burke's advice to post flyers around town.

"He's working really well on the longe line," she said. "He must have had some training, at least. He's a really pretty mover, so I think he'd be a great saddle seat horse." Saddle seat was Leslie's favorite style of riding, where the horse carries his head and neck in an upright posture and he lifts his knees and hocks high.

"Are you going to try riding him?"

Leslie shrugged. "I hadn't really thought of making training plans. I've just been assuming his owner would show up one of these days and want him back."

"Well, it's been a few weeks and no one has come forward. Why not see what he knows?"

Holly was always eager to try out a new horse, just like Leslie. Her enthusiasm was one of the things Leslie really liked about her.

"I was going to work him next. Maybe I could put a saddle on him and see how he does. Want to watch?"

"Sure. My lesson isn't for another hour. I asked mom to drop me off early so we could catch up."

Although Leslie, Holly and Alex went to the same school, they did not have any classes together that year. They didn't get to spend as much time together as they did the year before. It was their first year in high school and it was a big adjustment for Leslie to get used to the big school with twice as many students as her junior high.

"Great! Let's get him and put him in the cross ties. You can help me groom him."

They went to his stall. Leslie led Spark to the cross ties and she and Holly set to work. They took turns grooming him, Holly rubbing his coat vigorously with a rubber curry and Leslie following with the body brush, flicking off all the dead hair and dirt the curry brought out. Holly sprayed him with a conditioning spray that helped to moisturize his coat and bring back some of the shine, and Leslie rubbed him down with a soft cloth to rub in the conditioner and bring out his natural oils.

"All right, I think he's ready," Holly said after she cleaned out his hooves with a hoof pick. "Shall we get the saddle?"

"OK. Remember, we're just going to put it on him and longe him in it today to see how he takes it. Since we don't know how much training he has, it would be dangerous to try to just hop on and ride him. This will be a slow process over a few days."

Holly smiled and nodded. "I know. I'm just excited to see what he can do! I guess we don't want to get anyone hurt, though."

Leslie led the way into the tack room. "Right, and we

don't want to scare him or stress him out too much. He's been through quite an ordeal."

She selected a lightweight English saddle from one of the racks. It was one they often used on green horses, because it was old and could withstand rough treatment if the horse decided not to cooperate.

"Can you grab that saddle pad and a girth?" she asked, pointing to the items she wanted. Holly picked them up and followed Leslie out.

Leslie set the saddle on a rack next to the cross ties and took the girth and saddle pad from Holly.

"First, let's see how he reacts to the tack."

She laid the girth across the saddle and walked up to Spark to show him the pad. The gelding looked at it and sniffed it briefly, but did not widen his eyes or nostrils in fear.

"That's a good sign," Leslie said to Holly. "If he'd never seen one before, he probably would have reacted to it."

She gently reached out and rubbed the pad along Spark's neck. He did not flinch or move, so she laid it over his back and then picked up the saddle. When he reacted to it no more than he had the saddle pad, she placed it gently on his back and loosely buckled on the girth.

"Looks like he's done this before," Holly said. "He looks like he couldn't care less."

Leslie looked at her and smiled. "I think you're right. Dr. Burke thinks he's about eight years old, so it would make sense that he's had some training."

She tightened the girth a little and clipped a longe line onto Spark's halter before unclipping the ties.

"Here goes nothing!"

She led him into the arena and tightened the girth one

more time before clucking her tongue to him to walk in a circle around her. She stood in the middle and slowly played out the longe line until he was walking in a large circle, and then she clucked twice to tell him to trot. He swung into a trot like he had every other time she had longed him, unmindful of the saddle on his back or the stirrups that bounced around. Holly watched from the arena fence, resting her arms on the top rail.

Leslie longed Spark for ten minutes, asking him to trot and canter in both directions before telling him to halt.

"Well, that was easy!" she called to Holly. "I'm just going to walk him a little until he cools down. He's pretty warm."

"He looks good with a saddle," Holly called back. She checked her watch and added, "Uh oh, I only have fifteen minutes until my lesson. I'd better get Sundance ready!"

She ran down the barn aisle to get her horse, and Leslie walked Spark so he would slowly cool off. The air was chilly, and she did not want him to cool down too quickly and get sick. Because he was so emaciated when he arrived at Green Meadow, he had lost a lot of the muscle and fitness he should have had and ten minutes of longeing was a lot more work for him than it would be for a normal, fit horse.

When Spark had cooled off to Leslie's satisfaction, she cross tied him and untacked him, then groomed him thoroughly to remove any trace of sweat. He seemed to enjoy it, because he leaned into her while she worked.

"You sure are a good boy, Spark," Leslie told him. "I bet someone loved you very much at one time."

She offered him a couple of cookies, which he took gently but eagerly.

She led him to his stall and put him away. She was buckling his halter onto the bar on his door when Alex walked up to her.

"Hey, sunshine!" he said, beaming at her with his hazel eyes twinkling. "I saw you longe Spark with a saddle. Moving right along, eh?"

Leslie smiled back at him and gave him a quick kiss before answering, "He sure is. He's such a good boy; I bet he's already trained. I'm still going to take it slow, though."

"Good idea. No reason to push things. What are you going to do now?"

"I'm going to go out and tell Helen, I mean Mom, about how Spark did today. Then I need to get on my stalls. How about you?"

"I need to longe two horses. Then I get my lesson. Guess I'd better get to it."

"Yeah, get to work, you slacker," Leslie teased, ruffling his sandy brown hair with her fingers.

They kissed again before going their separate ways. Leslie thought about their first date when they were so shy they could barely look each other in the eye. Alex had given her a quick peck on the cheek before running off to his car. It was the first time either of them had been on a date, let alone in a relationship. It had taken them a few weeks to really feel comfortable with each other as boyfriend and girlfriend, but it had gotten to the point that she couldn't imagine not being with him.

She walked outside, blinking in the bright fall sunshine. She headed to the center of the outdoor arena, where Helen was standing while she gave Holly her lesson.

"Hi Mom," she said, grinning.

"Good, Holly! Now get your heels down. That's right." Helen shouted, and then she turned to Leslie. "Hi, sweetie! How's your morning going?"

"Well, good news and bad news," Leslie answered, frowning when she remembered what Dr. Burke had said.

"Uh oh. Give me the bad news first. Your left hand is lower than your right!" The last was shouted to Holly, who groaned and adjusted her hands. Leslie giggled; she knew that every rider, no matter how talented, had their problems they always struggled with.

"Dr. Burke isn't happy with Lucky's progress. She said I can start taking him for longer walks and take him outside a little, but that's all." Leslie sighed. "I'm worried about him."

Helen gave her a hug, then called out, "OK, Holly, let's do some work on your strength and balance. Drop your stirrups and do some laps of posting trot."

Holly stopped and took her feet out of her stirrups, then laid them over her saddle so they wouldn't flop around and hit her horse, Sundance, in the sides while he trotted. Then, she asked him to trot again and practiced her position without using the stirrups to keep her in the saddle.

Helen said to Leslie, "I know you are, and I am too. All we can do is hope for the best. At least you can take him for longer walks now; that's something. Was that the good news?"

"Part of it. I put a saddle on Spark today and longed him in it!" Leslie's spirits perked up when she thought of the happy-go-lucky way Spark approached his work.

"Oh, that's great! How did he do?" Louder, she called, "Good, Holly! Reverse and go the other way!"

"He was perfect! He must have had some training before, and he's really talented. He really loves people too. I think he must have meant something to someone once."

Helen smiled. "Just don't get too attached, Leslie. His real owner could show up at any time."

Leslie sighed. It seemed everyone felt the need to reminder her of that. "I know, Mom. I'll try not to get attached, but without Lucky to ride, it'll be nice to have another horse to concentrate on, you know?"

Helen looked at Leslie, studying her face. "That's fine. He's been here long enough that I'm sure his real owner won't mind you brushing him up on his training, if that's what you want to do. Just don't let your other duties slide, OK?"

"I promise I won't. In fact, I'd better go get to work on my chores."

Leslie waved to Holly and walked back into the barn to clean her share of the stalls. While she worked, she thought about Spark and Lucky, and what the future might hold for both of them.

Chapter Seven:
Halloween

Leslie hurried through the halls of her high school, pushing through the crowd. She needed to get to Holly's locker so she could drop off her invitation to the Green Meadow Halloween party before the bell rang for third period. She was almost there when someone stepped in front of her and halted her progress.

"Hello, Leslie."

It was Kate Wellesley, Leslie's rival at horse shows. Kate's parents had bred Lucky, Leslie's horse, but then left him at a livestock auction when they decided he did not meet their standards. Leslie had outbid a meat buyer, and Lucky had become hers.

Leslie sighed. She didn't have the time or energy to deal with Kate.

"Hello, Kate." She tried to brush past the other girl, but Kate stepped in front of her again.

"I hear you have a new horse at Green Meadow. Another loser you stole from its rightful owner?"

Leslie felt heat rising in her cheeks. Kate had a way of

bringing out the worst in her. "Kate, you know darned good and well that I did not steal Lucky. Your parents turned him over to the auction and signed over the papers. I bought him fair and square. Now, if you'll excuse me, I have to get to class."

She stepped around Kate, and that time Kate let her pass. When she was a few steps down the hall, she heard Kate laughing behind her. She shook her head in annoyance.

When Leslie reached Holly's locker at last, she pushed the invitation through the vents and hurried off to class. She arrived at her classroom door at the moment the bell sounded, and she pushed her way through it.

Her math teacher, Mr. White, glared at her while she made her way to her seat. "Pushing it a little close, aren't we, Miss Clark?"

Giggles surrounded Leslie and she sank into her chair.

"Now, if Miss Clark approves, shall we open our books and get down to business?"

He looked at her as though waiting for an answer, and Leslie nodded and pulled out her math book. Kate had succeeded in ruining Leslie's day yet again.

That afternoon, on the bus ride home from school, Leslie was able to see Alex at last. She had not seen him all day and was relieved to see he had already boarded the bus and saved her a seat so they could sit together.

"Boy am I glad to see you!" she exclaimed, flopping down in the seat next to him.

He gave her a quick peck on the cheek, but that was all, The bus driver, Mrs. Schmidt, tended to get irritable by overt displays of affection, and she had already yelled at them once that year to "Cool it!" when all they were doing was holding hands.

"Sounds like you didn't have a very good day. What happened?"

Leslie told him about her encounter with Kate and the resulting embarrassment from her math teacher.

Alex nodded solemnly. "That Kate. I don't know why she spends so much energy trying to get to you. You shouldn't give her the satisfaction of getting mad."

"I know, but it's hard not to react. She just makes me so angry! I don't know what she has against me."

Alex crinkled his brow, appearing to think about the problem for a moment before he answered.

"Remember how she kept trying to sabotage you during the show season? She was trying to keep you from beating her. I think she recognizes that you're a talented rider, and she's worried about it. It didn't help when you won the equitation class at Nationals this year and beat her."

Leslie considered what he said and nodded. "I'm sure you're right. I guess she just can't stand the fact that this poor girl can ride as well or better than she."

"I wonder how she heard about Spark," he mused.

"Maybe Dr. Burke asked her parents about him when she was trying to find his owner. I bet she's afraid I stumbled on a new superstar that's going to beat her in the show ring."

Leslie snickered at the thought of Kate being worried about Leslie beating her.

When the bus pulled up in front of Green Meadow a few minutes later, Leslie and Alex walked off together and walked up the driveway to the stable. They both had chores to do before dinner and homework.

"The Halloween party seems like it's going to be fun," Alex said while they walked. He had started working at Green Meadow only a few months before, so he would be attending the stable's Halloween party for the first time.

"Loads of fun. It's a big deal every year, and all the clients and their families come."

"I'm really looking forward to the haunted house. Holly said it was really scary last year."

"I was almost afraid to go in by myself! My dad, Juan and Josh have been making plans all month, and they won't breathe a word of their plans. When they start building it, no one will be allowed anywhere near it so they can keep it a surprise."

"Speaking of surprises, our costumes are going to be the best."

Alex and Leslie had been planning their costumes for over a month and were keeping them top secret so they could surprise their friends.

"I know! I can't wait. I think this is going to be my best costume yet!" Leslie was so excited at the thought of it that she skipped while she walked.

"Wait a minute," Alex said, stopping in the middle of the driveway. "What horse will you ride? I mean, since Lucky is still on the mend, and all..." his voice trailed off and he blushed, looking down at his feet.

Leslie stopped and turned to face him. "It's OK, Alex. You don't have to feel bad about mentioning it. You're right, I hadn't even thought of it. I'll figure out some-thing—after all, I live at a stable full of horses, don't I?"

When they reached the barn, they put their backpacks in the lounge and then went their separate ways. Alex had chores to do, and Leslie had horses to work. She went to

Lucky's stall first and gave him a thorough grooming and tended his hock wound. She then took him for a walk. He seemed to be in good spirits; his ears were pricked and his eyes were bright.

"Looks like you're feeling better today, boy," she told him, patting him affectionately on the neck. However, despite his apparent good mood, he still walked gingerly on his injured hind leg.

After she was done with Lucky, it was Spark's turn. Leslie put him in the cross ties and groomed him, then put the saddle on him. She looked him over and thought about what he would be like to ride. She had to have a horse for her Halloween costume; it would not work without one. She went into the tack room and picked out a bridle with a nice, smooth snaffle.

I won't ride him just yet, but I'll see how he reacts to the bit and if he knows how to steer and stop, she thought, walking back to Spark. Out loud she said, "OK, Spark. Let's see how you like this."

She unsnapped the cross ties from his halter, unbuckled his halter and fastened it around his neck. Then, she held the bridle in front of his face with her right hand and gently guided the bit into his hand with her left. He opened his mouth willingly and she slipped the bridle on over his ears. She adjusted the bridle to make sure it fit his head properly, and then she put the reins over his head and buckled them securely with the throatlatch strap on the bridle so they wouldn't droop.

She took two long longe lines off a nearby hook and clipped one to the bit on Spark's bridle and led him out to the center of the indoor arena. She dropped the extra longe line and picked up the longe whip and clucked to him to circle her at the walk. After longeing him for a few minutes in each direction, she brought him to a halt.

"OK, let's see if you know how to ground drive, Spark," she said.

She ran a line through each stirrup on the saddle and hooked them to the bit, then moved behind him. Making sure she was far enough behind him so he could not kick her if he decided he didn't like ground driving, she clucked to him and he walked forward. She walked along behind, steering him in circles, figure-eights, serpentines and all around the arena and occasionally asking him to stop. He did everything she asked willingly and confidently.

"You have definitely done this before," she told him, smiling. "No horse takes to this so easily the first time they do it."

She moved to the side of him and asked him to trot and canter in circles around her while she held the lines.

"So, you also know how to long line," she said thoughtfully. "I'd be willing to bet you've had under saddle training, too. Should I just hop on and try it?"

"Yes! I really want you to ride me!"

Leslie laughed at the high-pitched voice that came from behind her. She turned around to see Alex sitting on the fence.

"How did you sneak up on me like that?" she asked.

"I've been here for a couple of minutes. You aren't one for paying attention to your surroundings, are you?" he joked.

"Do you really think I should get on him?"

"Why not? He seems like he knows all this stuff already, so why wait?"

Leslie bit her lip. "I guess you're right. Would you mind getting my helmet out of the tack room while I take the lines off?"

Alex nodded and walked into the tack room, and Leslie unclipped the lines from Spark's bridle, rolled them up, and set them on the arena fence. Alex brought her helmet, she let down her stirrups and unbuckled the reins from under the throatlatch, where she had tied them up so they wouldn't slip off his head.

"Ready?" Alex asked.

"If not now, when?" she asked, gathering the reins in her hand.

She put her foot in the stirrup and bounced up and down a little. Spark did not move, so she pulled herself up and swung her leg over the saddle. The horse stood quietly, and the girl smiled triumphantly.

"Cool!" Alex said. "Looks like he doesn't care. How does he feel?"

"Good. I never noticed he was bigger than Lucky until I climbed up here."

"You look good on him. He's a good size for you, even better than Lucky."

Leslie squeezed Spark's sides with her legs and clucked to him to walk. She rode him for several minutes, walking around the arena in both directions and in circles. He followed every cue. She rode to the center of the arena and asked him to stop, and then she swung her leg over the saddle and jumped to the ground.

"That's it?" Alex asked. "You're not going to trot?"

"I don't want to push him too much," Leslie replied, running her stirrups up to the top of the leathers so they would not swing or catch on anything. "He's still regaining his strength from when he was starved, not to mention his scare with the fire."

She led him out of the arena and to the cross ties to

untack him.

Alex helped her. "So, how long do you think it'll take to get him up to speed?" he asked while they worked.

"I'll build him up slowly, doing a little more every day, and he should be in pretty good shape in a month or so."

An idea came to Leslie and she stopped what she was doing and stared at Alex.

"Alex, did anyone see me riding him today?"

Alex looked around. "No, I don't think so. Helen's outside, and no one came in while you were on him. Why?"

"I just had the best idea. What if I ride him at night, when no one else is around, and then use him for our Halloween costumes? Think how surprised everyone will be to see me riding him!"

Alex looked thoughtful. "I don't know, Leslie. Riding at night, alone? What if something happened to you? Isn't there, like, a rule about that?"

"I have my cell phone, so I can call for help if I need to. I'll tell Helen I'm spending time with Lucky so she doesn't wonder what I'm doing. It's only for a week. After the big surprise, I'll go legit. I promise."

Alex still didn't look like he agreed with her plan, but he nodded slowly. "All right, but call me every night when you're done so I know you didn't get your head splattered all over the arena, OK?"

"Deal," she said, sticking her hand out and shaking Alex's.

They grinned at each other, then Alex walked away to get Fred ready for his lesson. Leslie finished grooming Spark and put him away, then set off to work the horses she had been assigned for that day.

The next night, Leslie tried to calm her nerves at the dinner table while she waited for the right moment to tell her parents she needed extra barn time. She wasn't in the habit of lying, but she wanted her costume to be a surprise to everyone, including them. She and Alex had had to arrange for their costumes on the sly, and they were enjoying the anticipation of revealing their surprise the night of the party. However, not telling them about riding Spark was different; it was lying about what she was doing.

When she had eaten her last bite of dinner, she wiped her hands on her pants to dry them. "Um, is it OK if I spend some extra time with Lucky after dinner from now on? I'm feeling really bad for him, being stuck in his stall all the time."

She played with invisible bits of food on her plate with her fork as she spoke, unable to look her parents in the eye.

"I don't see why not," her father said. "If that's OK with you, Helen?"

"Sure," Helen answered, "as long as you don't neglect your homework."

"I promise!" Leslie said, happy her plan was working so far.

She walked out to the barn, zipping up her jacket and wrapping her arms around herself. The nights were getting colder, but the barn was insulated. She checked her pocket to make sure her cell phone was still there, and it was. She was a little nervous about riding an unfamiliar horse by herself at night, but knowing help was only a few steps and a phone call away calmed her nerves.

She let herself in through the access door and closed it behind her, then hurried to Spark's stall. She led him to the cross ties and groomed and tacked him up quickly.

"Let's get this over with, boy," she said. "I have homework to do, and I don't want to be out here by myself any longer than I need to be."

She longed him for a few minutes to warm him up and make sure he was not going to buck, then set the longe line aside and made sure her helmet was on tightly.

"Ready, Spark? You're not going to do anything silly and drop me in the dirt, are you?" He blinked at her benignly, so she mounted. "I guess you wouldn't tell me if you were planning something, would you?"

She squeezed her legs, and he stepped off into a walk. After walking for a few minutes in each direction, she shortened the reins and asked him to trot. He had a comfortable gait, with enough bounce to help her post but smooth enough that it was comfortable to ride.

She made some circles and figure eights at the trot, and then she asked Spark to walk, which he responded to obediently. She patted him on the neck and said, "You're a good boy, aren't you? You do everything I ask. I think someone must have put a lot of training into you."

His neck was warm to the touch and he panted a little, so Leslie decided he had had enough for one night. "We'll try cantering tomorrow night, boy," she told him.

She rode him around at the walk until he cooled down. She dismounted, then untacked and groomed him thoroughly but quickly before she led him back to his stall. Then she called Alex.

"Hey, it's me," she said when he answered.

"Hey, me," he joked. "How'd it go? Are you lying on the arena floor, legs horribly mangled, skull oozing brains and blood?"

Leslie smiled. "Nope, it went great. We trotted tonight, and he was just fine!"

"Well, congrats! Are you going in to work on your homework now?"

"Yep, and I have tons. See you tomorrow on the bus?"

"You bet!"

They hung up, and Leslie hurried to the house to do her homework, smiling to herself about her success with Spark.

"How was Lucky?" Helen called to her when Leslie walked past the living room.

"Oh, he was pretty much the same," Leslie said, hurrying up the stairs she wouldn't have to look anyone in the eye and lie any more that night.

Each night for the next week, Leslie went out to the barn after dinner to "visit with Lucky." Helen offered to keep her company once, but Leslie told her she was enjoying the alone time. She felt bad saying it, but if Helen came out, she would lose a night of riding Spark, and she needed all the time with him she could get if her Halloween costume was going to be a successful surprise.

Spark continued to behave, much to Leslie's relief. Each night they did a little bit more, and by the night before Halloween, he was trotting and cantering just like a show horse.

"I'm afraid I'm becoming a little attached to you, boy," she told him while she untacked him for the last time before the party. "I don't know what I'm going to do if your owner shows up."

He responded by nudging her with his muzzle and

she rubbed it gently. He gazed at her with his big brown eyes, and her heart melted.

"You are such a Romeo!" she told him.

The next day, everyone at the barn worked to prepare for the party. It was Saturday, so Leslie and Alex didn't have school. They worked together to decorate the barn inside and out with festive Halloween decorations, like orange and black paper streamers, bales of straw and the Jack O'Lanterns Alex had carved while Leslie was riding Spark every night. They pulled some tables and chairs out of the storage room and set them up behind the barn, where the party would be held, and Helen covered the tables with Halloween table cloths. She had already set up outdoor heaters and lamps.

"This place looks great!" Alex said, standing back and surveying their handiwork.

"You two did a great job," Helen said. "This will be a great party!"

Dan walked out of the house carrying a tray of sandwiches. He was catering the event. "Can you kids help me carry the rest of the stuff out of the house? It's all set out on the kitchen counters."

"Sure, Dad," Leslie said, and she and Alex hurried into the house. There were several trays set out with crackers and cheese and vegetables and dip. There were also bowls of chips and dips, fruit and cookies.

"Boy, your dad sure knows how to cater a party, doesn't he?"

Leslie nodded. "Yep. He loves to feed people. He's a great cook. He's catered a lot of Helen's parties."

By the time everything was set out and ready, it was almost time for the guests to arrive. "I guess we'd all better get into our costumes," Helen said, looking at her watch.

"We'll see you at the party in a little while," Leslie said. "We don't want you to see our costumes until just the right time!"

"Well, all right, but these better be some pretty great costumes with all this secrecy!" Helen said, chuckling.

Leslie made an X over her heart with her index finger. "Don't worry; our costumes are going to be the talk of the party!"

Helen and Dan went into the house to change while Alex and Leslie went to the barn. "OK, you take the tack room to change, and I'll take the office," Leslie said.

They retrieved their costumes from the little-used storage closet in the lounge, where they had hidden them, and went to their respective rooms to change. Although the curtains were drawn over the office window, Leslie could see lights from the arriving cars, and she could hear people laughing and talking when they walked by. When she was ready, she walked out into the barn aisle.

Alex was waiting for her, and she smiled appreciatively. "You look great!"

He let out a low whistle. "You do too! These costumes we rented are great."

"Let's go get the horses. I hope they don't freak out when they see us in these crazy get-ups," she said.

"Me too."

They retrieved Fred and Spark from their stalls and quickly tacked them up, then led them through the arena to the side door of the barn.

"It's a good thing the party's outside," Alex said. "Otherwise, I don't think we could have pulled this off."

"We've always had them outside. It just seems so festive to have the party outside, under the stars."

She mounted, and Alex handed her a Jack O'Lantern he had hidden by the door earlier in the day before he mounted Fred.

"Ready?" he asked, grinning through his makeup.

"Ready!" She replied.

Alex turned Fred toward the party and kicked him into a gallop, and Leslie followed a few yards behind, reins in one hand and Jack O'Lantern in the other. She could barely see through her costume, but was able to follow well enough. Alex turned the corner of the barn in front of her, and she heard surprised exclamations from the party goers. She rounded the corner and saw Alex was riding around the edge of the party as they had planned, while kids and adults alike pointed and whooped. Then it was her turn to canter by.

"Who is that, Daddy?" she heard a child yell in an excited voice.

"It's Ichabod Crane and the Headless Horseman!" he called back, and Leslie smiled. Their costumes had worked.

Just before she reached the edge of the party, Leslie pulled Spark to a stop. She wished she could make him rear for effect, but she would have to make do without it. She picked a spot where no one would get hit and threw the Jack O'Lantern, then wheeled Spark around and cantered away, around the next corner of the barn. Behind her, she heard the party goers burst into applause.

She pulled up in front of the barn, where Alex was waiting for her. "That was great!" he said, grinning from ear to ear.

"They loved it, and the horses did great!" Leslie answered, patting Spark on the neck. "Now let's get them untacked so we can go enjoy the party."

They worked quickly to put the horses away in their stalls. When finished, they walked to the party area, where they were greeted with applause. They stopped and bowed, grinning, and then people walked up to shake their hands. Leslie adjusted her cape around her real neck, instead of the fake one with the supposedly severed head, so she could see and talk to people normally.

When Helen reached them, dressed as a nurse, her face was tight and her words measured. "Leslie, that was great, but was that Spark you were riding?"

Leslie felt her stomach turn over; Helen did not usually use that tone with her. "Yes, but he was really good..."

"We'll talk about this later," Helen said curtly and walked away.

She was replaced at Leslie's side by Holly, who was dressed as Red Riding Hood and grinning from ear to ear.

"You guys, that was so cool! Everyone was totally surprised. How did you pull it off?"

"We rented costumes in town," Alex explained. Leslie guessed he had not been paying attention when Helen spoke to her, because he was still laughing and happy, while she felt horrible.

Maybe this big surprise wasn't such a good idea, she thought. She didn't want to ruin the party for her friends, though, so she pasted a smile on her face and tried to match Holly's enthusiasm.

"Yeah, and I practiced on Spark at night to get him ready and keep it a surprise," she said.

"Well, it worked! Come on, let's go get something to eat." Holly grabbed Leslie's sleeve and pulled her toward the food table while Alex followed along behind. However, Leslie had completely lost her appetite.

For the rest of the night, Leslie tried to enjoy the party. She visited with her friends from the barn, with whom she rarely had the opportunity to talk because she was so busy taking care of the horses. She forced herself to eat, she drank punch, and she and Alex danced when somebody turned up the stereo. After a while, she managed to forget she was in trouble and enjoyed herself.

Kids took turns going through the haunted house Dan, Juan and Josh had built, and Leslie and Alex went together. They screamed together when spiders dropped from the ceiling or mummies jumped out of coffins, held each other tightly while walking through the maze of cobwebs, and shuddered together when they walked past the real pig's head, covered in flies.

"That was great!" Alex said. "Let's do it again!"

"Not on your life!" she told him. "You go. I'm going to go think about ponies and rainbows and other harmless things."

All in all, she had a good time, but when Helen avoided her, Leslie felt as though she had a rock in her stomach that would not wash away, even with the gallons of punch she drank. Leslie knew Helen was not happy with her, and Leslie would have to answer for her actions. She just hoped Helen would not be so angry as to ground her or keep her from riding Spark again.

It was not until most of the guests had left and they were cleaning up that Helen approached Leslie. Her face and voice, which had been carefully neutral during Leslie's brief exchange with her during the party, was now laced with anger.

"Leslie, would you care to explain how it is that your

performance included a stray horse that we did not even know for sure was broke to ride?"

Helen's hands were balled into fists on her hips.

Leslie held up her hands in a placating gesture, or a defensive one, she was not sure which. "Mom, it's totally OK. I worked with him on the longe line first, and when he ground drove like he knew what he was doing, I decided to hop on him and he was fine. Alex was there in case something went wrong, but it didn't. I've been riding him every night for the past week to make sure he would be ready."

Leslie felt deflated. The fun surprise she and Alex had worked so hard for was suddenly anything but fun.

"All this time that you told me you were spending extra time with Lucky, you were actually riding a strange horse? What if you'd been hurt? You know riding by yourself is against the rules!"

Helen was really angry by that time, her face turning red with emotion.

The lies Leslie had told all week, which had been told in the name of good fun at the time, now weighed heavily on her.

She looked down at her feet and answered, "I wanted it to be a surprise. I always brought my cell phone with me in case something happened, and I called Alex every night when I was done so he would know I was OK."

Helen turned to Alex, who was busily cleaning up a table nearby — almost too busily, as though he was trying to cover up the fact that he was listening.

"You knew about this, and you let her do it? I thought you knew better." Alex shrank away from her scolding, and she looked back at Leslie with narrowed eyes. "I thought you both did."

"I'm sorry," Leslie said in a small voice. "I thought it would be a fun surprise, but I guess I was wrong."

"You're very lucky nothing horrible happened, Leslie. You could have been seriously injured, and it would have been hours before anyone thought to look for you. Don't you ever do that again, do you understand me?"

Leslie nodded, and Helen suddenly wrapped her arms around her step daughter in a fierce hug, which Leslie returned with relief.

"All that said, Leslie, I am proud of you for doing such a good job with him, and you were the talk of the party. I want to hear all about it later, OK?"

Leslie sniffed and answered, "It's a deal."

Helen pulled away, placing her hands on Leslie's shoulders and looking intently at her. "I should probably punish you, but it's not often you do anything you shouldn't. I'm going to let you off with a warning; does that sound fair?"

Leslie sighed with relief and nodded vigorously. "Very fair, thank you! So, can I keep riding Spark?"

Helen signed and shrugged. "I don't see why not. We don't know if his real owner will ever show up, and he seems broke enough to me. You might as well keep working with him, if that's what you want to do. Just don't let it get in the way of your other duties or your homework, and never again after barn hours, OK?"

"Of course not. Besides, as long as Lucky is laid up, I'm not doing very much with him. At least I have a horse to ride while I wait for him to get better."

Although there were school horses at the barn, they already had a job—giving lessons to riding students. Leslie could ride them every once in a while, but not on a regular basis.

"All right, now that that's settled, let's get to work cleaning this place up. What a mess!"

"What a party!" said Alex, and Leslie agreed. The best part was that the rock in her stomach was finally gone.

Chapter Eight:
November

With the passing of Halloween, the days grew shorter and colder. The horses were warm in their thick winter coats, requiring them to be body clipped so they wouldn't overheat when worked. Riders wore layers to keep warm. Riding lessons moved to the indoor arena, out of the wind and rain, which made the arena more crowded. Leslie had to constantly keep an eye out for other riders while she worked her horses.

She rode Spark every day, and Helen watched approvingly. Leslie had told her about the ground work she had done with him before riding him, and how she built him up slowly so he would not be too stressed about his work.

Helen had approved of Leslie's progress. "You did everything just right, Leslie. With the exception of lying to your parents and riding at night by yourself, of course." She had said the last part with a smile. "I think you will make a fine trainer one day."

Leslie had been elated at the compliment. "Thank you! Of course, I had a pretty good teacher," she had, winking.

Helen had rolled her eyes. "Sucking up will get you nowhere!"

Spark progressed well, and it became increasingly evident that he had had extensive training at some point in his life.

"Do you think he was somebody's show horse?" Alex asked one day while he watched Leslie ride.

"He acts like it, doesn't he? But if he were, I would think we would recognize him. We go to all the local shows, and surely he would have been there." Leslie answered. She added, "I wonder if whoever abandoned him lived far away and trailered him to wherever they let him go?"

Alex rubbed his chin thoughtfully. "Yeah, or maybe he was turned loose hundreds of miles away and he wandered here all by himself. Remember that movie where the dog went all the way across the country?"

"I don't know, Alex. Why would he travel so far from home all by himself? In the movie, the dog was following his owners, or was lost miles from home. I can't remember which. Anyway, he had a reason to go all that way. Besides, that was just a movie."

"I guess that's true. Still, it's an interesting mystery. It's too bad we don't know who he is though, so you could get his papers. He'd be a great show horse."

"I know. Sadly, no matter how much he looks like an Arabian, I can't show him at Arabian horse shows unless I have his registration papers. I guess I could show him at schooling shows, though. It will still be fun."

A week after Halloween, Dr. Burke visited again to

check on Lucky. After examining him, she said, "Well, I hate to tell you this, Leslie, but we should have seen more improvement by now. I'm afraid he's probably never going to be a hundred percent better."

Leslie's heart fell. She had suspected in the preceding weeks that Lucky would not get better, because he improved so slowly. He no longer limped, but he took short steps on the injured leg and moved slowly. However, hearing the confirmation of her fears made it much more real.

Leslie was too overcome with emotion to speak. Dr. Burke hugged her and said, "Don't beat yourself up over this, Leslie. You couldn't have prevented it, and we did everything we could to make him better.

"I think the best thing for him would be to put him in the pasture with some horses he gets along well with and let him just live the good life. We can check him again in a few months, but the most work he's ever likely to be able to do again is a leisurely trail ride.

"I'm sorry, Leslie. I know how much he meant to you as a show horse."

Leslie wiped away the tears and swallowed.

"Thank you, Dr. Burke." It was a great effort to control her voice. "I know you did everything you could."

She led Lucky out to the pasture where the retired lesson horses lived, talking to him all the way about how much he would enjoy living in the pasture, and that she would go out and visit him often. She wondered who she was really trying to reassure: the horse or herself.

"Maybe in the spring we can go for a little trail ride now and then," she told him. "You'll like that. For now, you just concentrate on enjoying life and getting better, OK?"

Lucky's ears pricked up and he quickened his pace, obviously happy to be going out to the pasture. When Leslie led him inside and removed his halter, he immediately lay down and rolled, and then walked stiff-legged to the nearest patch of grass and began to eat heartily.

Two old geldings wandered over to say hello. The three horses sniffed each other, laid back their ears and swished their tails, then resumed eating as though nothing out of the ordinary were happening. None of them even flicked an ear in Leslie's direction.

"Nice to know you're as heartbroken about this as I am, Lucky!" Leslie couldn't help smiling at how quickly and enthusiastically Lucky had taken to his new lifestyle.

She stood and watched him for several minutes, then turned and walked back to the barn.

Julie was standing in the tack room when Leslie went in.

"What did Dr. Burke say about Lucky?" the assistant trainer asked. When Leslie explained, Julie hugged her and said, "I'm so sorry, Leslie. I hope some time off and rest does the trick so you can have him back soon."

"Thanks, Julie. I guess I've known ever since it happened that this could be the outcome, but I was hoping he would get better. I just hope he recovers enough for the occasional trail ride or something. I miss riding him."

"I'm sure you do. You two went through a lot together. At least you have Spark to ride now, right?"

Leslie smiled, thinking of him. "Yes, and I'm really enjoying working with him. He has a really good work ethic and does everything I ask of him. And he's really sweet, following me around and wanting affection all the time."

"Sounds like he has a great personality," Julie said

with a smile.

"Definitely."

The last week of November marked the arrival of Thanksgiving, one of Leslie's favorite holidays. Her parents didn't have any family in the area, so the holiday had always been a quiet affair with just the three of them. After Claire died, there had just been Dan and Leslie. He still cooked a full turkey dinner every year, and they enjoyed the leftovers for days afterward.

It was their first Thanksgiving with Helen, and they had agreed to spend it with just the three of them like Dan and Leslie were used to. Dan spent several days preparing, making pies, thawing the turkey and shopping for just the right ingredients. On Thanksgiving morning, he got out of bed at four o'clock to start cooking the turkey.

Leslie slept in until eight, and then walked out to the barn with Helen to feed the horses. Since it was a holiday, all of the help and the horses had the day off, but the horses still needed to be fed.

"I'm just warning you, Mom, don't go anywhere near the kitchen today. Dad is very territorial when it comes to cooking big meals like this. And he has knives in there, so you don't want to cross him!"

Helen laughed. "Was he like this with your mother, too?"

"For as long as I can remember."

They worked together to feed the horses, piling hay and grain into the small trailer they pulled with a golf cart. Leslie had mastered the art of driving the golf cart a couple of years before, so she climbed into the driver's seat and drove around the property to feed the horses while Helen rode in the passenger seat.

"The sound of horses calling for their breakfast is one of the most wonderful sounds in the world, don't you think?" Leslie asked. All around them, horses nickered and tossed their heads, waiting for their food.

"It sure is. Sometimes, I miss feeding the horses, because I love it so much. Of course, I wouldn't trade in my barn help for the world!"

By the time they finished feeding and walked back into the house, the air inside was filled with the delicious smell of roasting turkey and all kinds of other delicious smells. The dining room table was laid out with French toast, sausages and fresh-squeezed orange juice.

"What a surprise!" Helen exclaimed, eyeing the feast.

"I told you we're not allowed in the kitchen," Leslie said with a wink. "You didn't think he would let us starve, did you?"

"Let the two most important women in my life starve? Never!" Dan walked through the kitchen door, a pot of coffee in one hand and a pitcher of cream in the other. "Your timing is perfect. Let's sit down and eat before everything gets cold."

"You don't have to ask me twice!" Leslie said, dropping into her seat. She used her fork to help herself to French toast and sausage, then took a sip of her orange juice. "Mmmm. This juice is wonderful, Dad."

"My compliments to the chef!" Helen said, spearing a piece of sausage on her fork and raising it in salute.

Leslie and Dan followed suit, and the three clinked sausage links.

"To family... and being together," Dan said, and Leslie and Helen echoed him.

Once they finished eating, Dan stood and piled the

plates on top of each other. "Now, you two deserve a day off. You go have fun and leave these to me. Do whatever it is horsey girls do together."

Leslie and Helen looked at each other and shrugged. Neither of them was used to having a day completely free. "Trail ride?" Helen suggested.

"Why not? The trails aren't as pretty as they used to be, but it will still be fun."

They dressed in warm clothing and walked down to the barn. While Leslie tacked up Spark, Helen tacked up Fred. They put on their helmets, mounted and were soon on their way. Despite the chill, the sky was a lovely shade of blue, and the air smelled fresh and clean. It had rained the day before, but all of the clouds had already cleared away.

Leslie drew in a big breath and let it out, enjoying the fresh air.

"I just love the weather we have here in California," she said. "In other places around the country, I bet they already have snow on the ground."

"Yep, and it might even be too cold to ride. Here, we have the luxury of being able to ride and show all year."

"Yes, that is one of the many things I'm thankful for," Leslie said, looking at Helen and smiling.

Helen smiled back. "Me too. Speaking of schooling shows, the Lost Lake Riders has their winter schooling show series. I was thinking of seeing if any of the students want to go. Want to take Spark?"

"Really? Do you think it's a good idea?"

"I don't see why not. He's going really well for you, and maybe someone there will recognize him. It's worth a shot, and if not, at least you can get him out and enjoy him."

Leslie grinned. "Sounds great!" She patted Spark's neck, then asked him, "What do you think, boy? Want to be in a horse show?" Spark snorted and bobbed his head, and she laughed.

Despite the fact that much of the forest was charred and bare, Leslie and Helen enjoyed their ride. The horses seemed to enjoy being out on the trail as well, prancing friskily from time to time. When they reached a part of the trail that was a long straightaway, they kicked their horses into a gallop and ran, whooping and laughing until they were breathless.

They pulled up their horses, and Helen said between breaths, "I guess we'd better head back. If we're gone too long, your dad might send out a search party for us."

She grinned, and Leslie grinned back.

"I guess you're right. The walk back should be just enough to cool the horses out."

They turned their horses' noses toward the barn and rode home at a leisurely pace. Despite the run, or perhaps because of it and the cold air, the horses were still fresh. They walked with their ears pricked up and a lively spring to their step, seeming to enjoy being out on a relaxing trail ride, rather than the hard work of riding in an arena and practicing for shows.

"Are you going to call Alex today?" Helen asked while they rode.

"He told me he'd call me after dinner. His family eats a little later than we do, so it'll be later tonight."

They rode in silence for a few minutes, before Leslie asked, "We haven't really talked about how you're liking the married life. Does it feel weird?"

"It did for the first month or so, but I'm settling in now. It's nice to have people in the house again—living by myself was pretty lonely—and it's really nice having a cook in the house! How about you? Are you feeling more at home now?"

Leslie thought for a moment before answering, "It was weird living in y our house at first. I kept turning the wrong way to go to the bathroom. Now, though, I really like it. I miss our old house sometimes, but now that we've put out some of our art and knickknacks and stuff, it's kind of a happy medium. And, I really love being able to walk outside and see the horses any time I want!"

"That is pretty nice. Before I bought this place, I had to commute to the horses every day and it got pretty old. It's also really nice having you around every day to help out. And I'm really impressed with how you've kept your grades up, even with your added responsibilities at the barn."

Leslie blushed. "Thanks. I've had some late nights keeping up with my homework, but it's worth it."

They rode into the barnyard and dismounted, then led their horses inside. By the time they untacked their horses and gave them a thorough grooming, it was time to go inside and clean up for dinner.

When Leslie opened the front door of the house and walked in, she was hit by a wave of warm air that smelled richly of turkey, gravy, stuffing and sweet potatoes.

"Mmmm! That is just the most heavenly scent ever," Leslie sighed.

"Even better than the smell of horses?" Helen teased.

Leslie laughed. "As much as I love the smell of hors-es, I have to say I love this more!"

Dan poked his head out of the kitchen. "Dinner is in half an hour, girls. Just enough time for showers. I don't want the smell of horse manure to compete with my masterpiece!"

"No problem!" Leslie said, and she and Helen hurried upstairs to shower and change.

After riding in the chilly autumn air, the hot shower warmed her down to her bones. Once she made sure she was clean from head to toe, she turned off the water, dried off and wrapped herself in her favorite fluffy robe.

She had laid out her outfit earlier in the day, a matching top and skirt in a soft brown that she thought was appropriate for the season. It was not often that she dressed up or even wore a skirt, and she wanted to look nice for the occasion of her first Thanksgiving with Helen.

She blew her thick hair dry and brushed it out so it fell elegantly around her shoulders and put the horseshoe-shaped earrings her father had given her for her birthday in her ears, and then put on her outfit and stepped into some sandals before walking downstairs.

Dan was putting the final touches on the table when she walked into the dining room, and he whistled at her.

"You look lovely, honey!"

Leslie blushed and dropped her eyes. "Thanks, Dad. You look great, too."

Somehow, he had found the time to change into a fresh dress shirt and a tie with turkeys on it.

"You're both a sight for sore eyes." Helen's voice sounded from over Leslie's shoulder.

Leslie turned to see Helen posing on the stairs, wearing a striking green dress that accentuated her figure. Dan whistled again, and Helen giggled while she walked down the remaining steps, balanced perfectly in her elegant black pumps. Leslie sighed, wishing she could look that sophisticated and poised.

Dan met Helen at the bottom of the stairs, took her

hands in his and gave her a brief but romantic kiss.

I wonder if Alex and I will ever be that sophisticated, Leslie wondered.

She glanced at the table. "Shall we all sit down?" she asked.

"We shall!" Dan said, offering an arm each to Helen and Leslie. He escorted them to their seats, pulling out first Helen's chair and then Leslie's.

"Your father really is quite the gentleman, you know," Helen said with a smile.

"Yes, he is. It's just one of the things I'm thankful for."

Dan winked and said, "Speaking of which, Leslie and I have a tradition of saying what we have been thankful for over the past year before we begin eating. Are you game, Helen?"

"Definitely, and I'll start. I'm thankful that the two of you have become such an important part of my life. I can't imagine living without either of you."

"Hear, hear!" Dan said, and the three clinked their glasses together in a toast. While the adult glasses were filled with wine, Leslie's held soda. "I think we can all agree on that one. Is there something else you're thankful for, Leslie?"

"I'm thankful for my work with the horses, and that I get to live my dream every day to work with them," Leslie responded, smiling. The three clinked their glasses again.

"And I'm thankful for my promotion at work," Dan said, and they toasted one more time. "All right, now let's dig in!"

Helen held up her hand to stop them. "Can we make one more toast before we start?"

"Of course!" Dan answered.

Helen held up her glass and quietly said, "To Claire."

Leslie's eyes misted over when she lifted her own glass and answered, "To Mom" at the same time Dan raised his and said, "To Claire."

Everyone was silent for a moment, lost in their own thoughts, until Dan cleared his throat and said huskily, "Ahem, well, she certainly wouldn't want us to eat cold dinner, now would she?"

For the next few minutes, the only sound in the dining room was that of silverware meeting porcelain, requests to pass this or that, and appreciative murmurs.

"Dan, you've outdone yourself. This turkey is the moistest, most delicious turkey I've ever tasted," Helen said, raising her glass of wine in Dan's direction.

Leslie took a sip of her soda. "Yeah, Dad, it's really good. Did you prepare it differently this year?"

Dan swallowed the food he was chewing. "Yes, I tried something new I saw on one of the cooking shows I like to watch. I brined the turkey, meaning I soaked it overnight in water, salt and spices. The brining process locks the juices into the meat, so that has a lot to do with how juicy and flavorful it is. I also basted it with a basting sauce made from Marsala wine and butter."

"Well, that sounds a lot more advanced than anything I've ever done," Helen quipped, chuckling. "At my family's Thanksgiving celebrations, all I'm allowed to bring is drinks."

Leslie laughed at that. Helen was not a bad cook, although she did not prepare anything fancy. She had cooked for Leslie a few times before when Leslie had spent the night when her father was out of town. Once Dan and Leslie moved in, however, Dan took over all the cooking duties.

When each of them had eaten as much as they could and more, one by one they each pushed their plates away and groaned.

"I don't know why I always eat so much on Thanksgiving," Dan said. "I just can't seem to stop myself, but I always regret it. Ooh, my stomach!" Despite his words, he grinned and rubbed his belly in appreciation.

"You eat so much for the same reason I do," Leslie said with a smile. "Because it's all so good, you just can't stop!"

"Hear, hear!" Helen said, raising her glass. She looked at it, appeared to think better of drinking any more to add to her large dinner, and put her glass back down on the table with a grimace.

"OK, you two sit here and digest for a minute," Leslie said, standing and pushing her chair in. "I'll start clearing the dishes and fill the dishwasher."

"Well, thank you, Leslie!" Dan answered. "Once you get a little bit of the disaster under control, I'll take care of the leftovers."

"Mmm, I think that's my favorite part about Thanksgiving," Helen said. "The leftovers. Since I've never had Thanksgiving dinner at my own house before, I haven't had turkey dinner leftovers since I stopped living with my parents."

"Dad has all kinds of great recipes for fixing them, too," Leslie said before she walked into the kitchen with a pile of plates. Leslie smiled while she worked, clearing the dirty dishes and filling the dishwasher. She enjoyed the quiet, homey Thanksgiving dinner with her parents. She heard bits and pieces of the conversation from the dining room: normal, everyday conversation of a married couple.

Normally Leslie hated doing dishes, especially after

such a big meal, but this time she enjoyed it. It gave her time to think about the events of the day, which led her back to the events of the year. She had gone from being the charity case at Green Meadow, with no horse of her own and working to pay for her lessons, to owning her own horse and winning a National Championship.

Then her father and Helen had married, and Leslie felt as though she had everything she ever wanted. She still worked at the barn, but she was paid for her efforts and she no longer had to pay for board or lessons since she was part of the family. Between that and her father's promotion at work, they lived much more comfortably than they did before.

Once everything was cleaned up, Helen suggested they go to a movie, one of her favorite Thanksgiving traditions.

"Sounds like a great idea! Leslie, do you want to see if Alex can join us, and I'll see what's playing?"

Leslie made the call, and was pleased to learn that Alex was able to join them.

"This is getting to be a regular thing," Dan said with a chuckle. "These double dates."

"You know, Dan, maybe the kids would like to have some alone time," Helen said thoughtfully. Looking at Leslie, she added, "If you two want to sit apart from us at the movie that would be OK."

She smiled and slipped her arm under Dan's while she said it, cuddling close to her new husband.

Leslie laughed. "Are you saying that for my benefit or yours?"

"Well, maybe a little of both."

They picked up Alex a short time later and Dan drove them to the movies. He splurged, buying large tubs of popcorn and soda, even though they didn't think they could eat another bite after Thanksgiving dinner. "It's not a movie without popcorn," Dan said.

They split up when they went inside the theater, Dan and Helen to find seats on the left side and Alex and Leslie to the right.

"At least we're far enough apart that we can kind of feel alone," Alex said.

"I know. I love my parents, but sometimes it's nice to just be alone with you!" Leslie responded. She looked at him and smiled.

"Ditto. It seems like there's always someone else around when we're together, and we haven't gotten to go out on many dates by ourselves."

Just then, the previews started and they snuggled together in silence to watch. At the end of the night, all agreed it was the nicest Thanksgiving any of them had in a long time.

Chapter Nine:
Christmas Formal

Leslie shouldered her way onto the bus, struggling to get herself and her backpack up the steps and down the aisle to where Alex waited for her. It was the Monday after Thanksgiving and the long weekend.

"Whew!" she said when she flopped down next to him. "These buses are not made for high school backpacks!"

"I know what you mean." He handed her a flyer while he spoke.

She looked it over. "Christmas Formal," she read out loud. "A dance?"

"Yeah. I was kind of thinking it might be fun to go. You know, get dressed up in clothes that don't belong in a barn and everything. We could have dinner and then go to the dance."

Leslie was surprised at the hopeful look in his eyes when he spoke, a look that was accompanied by a shrug and a tone that was almost too casual.

"Really? I didn't know you liked to dance. I don't really know how, but it sounds like fun!"

"So, you'll go? I don't know how to dance either, so we'll look stupid together." A small amount of enthusiasm crept into his voice, and Leslie had to keep herself from snickering at his attempt to look cool.

"What girl could turn down the chance to dress up and look stupid dancing?" She smiled and nudged him with her elbow.

"Great! I'll get the tickets tomorrow and make dinner reservations and everything. Mom said she'd drive us."

Leslie chuckled. "Sounds like you've been planning this already! What if I said no?"

"Aw, I figured I'd talk you into it somehow. I'm not above resorting to blackmail."

Leslie's eyes widened. "What could you possibly have on me to blackmail me with?" she asked.

Alex shrugged. "I don't know. I'd come up with something."

Leslie laughed again. "Well, all right then. I have to ask my parents, of course."

"Do you want to see if Holly and her boyfriend want to join us? We could double date."

"That would be fun. Todd is fun to hang out with, even if he doesn't really like horses."

"Maybe Holly will bring him around some day."

"I hope so," Leslie mused, "otherwise `I don't know how it will ever work out!"

The conversation turned to the subject of school. Leslie loved that time every afternoon, when they had the opportunity to just sit and talk about their day, their classes and all the crazy things that happen at school. It was a chance to unwind before going to the barn and starting her work there. Also, although they were surrounded by rowdy kids, they kept to themselves and Leslie felt like she had Alex all to herself for a while.

All too soon, the bus had arrived at Alex's stop. He did not go to the barn on Mondays, so Leslie would be spending the rest of the trip home alone. When she arrived, she hurried into the house to change, and then hurried out to the barn. She found Helen in the office, paying bills for the barn.

"Mom, guess what!" Leslie exclaimed, rushing into the office.

"What?" Helen asked, looking up from her work. She had been frowning in concentration when Leslie walked in, but from her sudden smile, Leslie guessed her stepmother welcomed the interruption.

"There's a Christmas formal at school in a couple of weeks. Alex asked me, and he said he'd take me to dinner before. Can I go?"

Helen's smile broadened. "Well, it's fine by me, but we should ask your father when he gets home before you plan on it, OK?"

"Of course! I'll ask him during dinner."

Helen bit the end of her pen and looked thoughtful for a moment. "This is your first dance, isn't it? I don't remember your going to any others."

"Nope, I've never been to one. They had them in junior high, but I never really had anyone to go with."

"Well, we'll have to go shopping, I suppose. It's a formal, so you'll need a dress. Would you mind if I was the one who took you shopping for your first formal dress?" Helen's eyes sparkled when she asked.

"Mind? Of course I don't mind! I would love it!"

"Well, I think it sounds like fun. We can go this weekend, if your father is fine with it all. Right now, though, you'd better let me get back to work or I won't get these bills paid."

"Thanks Mom! I have to get to work myself."

She stepped outside the office to check the board and saw that she had two horses to longe before she could ride Spark, so she hurried to her tasks.

That night at dinner, Leslie waited until everyone was settled and eating before she broached the subject of the dance. For some reason, she felt more nervous asking her father for permission than she had about asking Helen, even though he rarely said no to her.

She cleared her throat. "So, Dad, there's something I wanted to talk to you about," she began, stirring the mashed potatoes on her plate with her fork.

"Sure, honey. What is it?" he asked, cutting his meat like it was just any ordinary dinner.

Leslie looked at Helen, who winked at her in encouragement. Leslie cleared her throat, took a deep breath and announced, "There's a Christmas formal at school in a couple of weeks, and Alex asked me to go with him and have dinner before, and I would really like to go. May I?" She had said it all in one breath and had to inhale sharply at the end. She held her breath until her father answered.

He chewed thoughtfully, appearing to think it over. "A dance, huh? With a boy?"

Leslie rolled her eyes. "Yes, Dad. Alex is a boy, and we would be going to the dance together."

"I see. And would this boy be touching you while you dance?"

"Dad!"

He chuckled. "Well, all right. I guess one little dance

can't hurt. I guess you'll be wanting to go shopping for a dress or something, huh?"

"I already told her I'd take her," Helen said, then clapped her hand over her mouth, looking guilty.

"So, you already knew about this monstrosity and agreed to it?" he asked in mock anger.

Helen lifted her chin in mock defiance. "I did, and I told her it was OK with me if it was OK with you, and I told her I'd take her shopping. There, I said it! And I'm not sorry!"

"Well, what if I want to take her shopping myself?"

"Are you kidding? You'd buy her the ugliest old lady dress you could find. Forget it!" Helen answered, jabbing her fork at him for emphasis.

Dan rolled his eyes and said, "Women!" and they all laughed.

After dinner, Leslie called Alex to tell him she could go to the dance, and then she called Holly to see if she wanted to double date.

"I'd love to, but Todd hasn't asked me yet," Holly said.

"Do you think he will?"

"I don't know. He doesn't really like dressing up or dancing or anything like that." Leslie thought her friend sounded sad.

"Well, don't give up hope. I didn't know Alex liked that stuff, but he asked."

"Yeah, we'll see. I kind of hinted about it, though, and he just shrugged it off. He didn't seem like he cared."

"Maybe you should just ask him," Leslie suggested. "Tell him you really want to go, and there's no one you'd rather go with than him. Maybe he'll say yes just to make you happy."

"I don't know. He doesn't really like it when I ask him to do things. He likes to be the one to decide what we do."

Leslie was taken aback. "Really? I didn't realize that about him. Pretty old fashioned, don't you think?"

"Yeah, I guess so. He says that's the way it's supposed to be, because that's the way his parents are."

"That doesn't make it right, Holly. My dad and Helen aren't that way, and it wasn't that way with my real mom, either. They made decisions together."

"Anyway, let me wait to see if he asks me. If he does, maybe he'll want to double date. I'll let you know."

They said their goodbyes and hung up, and Leslie went up to her room to do homework. She was distracted, however, thinking about Holly and Todd and how different their relationship was from hers and Alex's or her parents.

"I'm starting to wonder what she sees in him," Leslie murmured aloud to her empty bedroom.

For the rest of the week, Leslie asked Holly every day after school if Todd had asked her to the dance, and every day Holly said no. On Saturday, Holly had her riding lesson, and Leslie kept her company while she tacked up Sundance.

"He still hasn't asked you, huh?" Leslie asked. "Mom's taking me dress shopping tomorrow and I thought we could go together."

"No, and I'm starting to think he's not going to. In fact, he was talking about going to some horror movie that night instead."

Leslie studied Holly's face.

She looks really unhappy, she thought.

Out loud, she asked, "I thought you hated horror movies?"

Holly shrugged and looked away. "I do, but he likes them, so what can I do?"

Leslie's mouth fell open. This was not the Holly she had known for several years. Holly had always been self-confident before.

I think I'm over my head, she thought. *I don't know how to deal with this.*

"Well, have a good lesson, Holly. I need to go take care of some things."

Leslie walked away, chewing her lower lip in thought. When she saw Julie coming out of a horse's stall, Leslie decided to see if older girl could help. Julie was twenty and had been in relationships before.

"Julie, do you have a few minutes? I really need to talk to someone about this, and Mom's busy teaching lessons."

Julie closed the stall door behind her and buckled the horse's halter on the bar on the door. "Sure, Leslie, what's up?"

Leslie looked over her shoulder at Holly, who was finished getting Sundance ready and leading him into the arena.

"It's Holly. She's seeing this guy, Todd. At first I thought he was pretty cool, but from what she tells me, he seems like kind of a jerk, and I'm a little worried about her."

Julie started walking toward a stall further down the barn aisle and motioned for Leslie to follow her.

"So, what makes you think he's a jerk? What's he doing?"

"Well, there's this dance coming up next week, and Holly really wants to go, and he doesn't."

"Lots of boys don't like dances, Leslie. That doesn't necessarily mean he's a jerk."

"Well, it's not just that. She said he wants to go to some horror movie that night instead, even though Holly really doesn't like horror movies."

"Sounds kind of insensitive, but hardly call for concern, Leslie. You're pretty lucky in that you and Alex have the same taste in a lot of things, but not every couple is like that."

Julie took a halter of a stall door and went inside to halter the horse.

Leslie bit her lip; she knew she wasn't getting the point across very well, but she tried again. "Well, it's something more than that, though. She said she can't ever ask him to do things when they go out, because he's old fashioned and says the man should make all the decisions, because that's how his parents are. And — well, you know Holly. She's usually really perky and happy, and lately she's been really quiet and reserved. It's — weird."

Leslie lapsed into silence, miserable, unsure how to make Julie understand what her gut knew was wrong.

Julie looked a little less skeptical, nodding thoughtfully. "Well, if you like, I can talk to her. It doesn't sound dangerous, necessarily, but it doesn't really sound healthy, either."

Leslie sighed in relief. "Thank you, Julie. Maybe she'll listen to you. I don't want to see her unhappy."

"No problem. I'll talk to her after her lesson, OK?"

Leslie went back to work, thinking about her friend the whole time. She had never really thought before about how lucky she was to have a boyfriend who liked a lot of the same things she did.

I'd like to think that even when we come across something we don't agree on, he'll at least respect my perspective, she thought.

Leslie was working a horse when Holly's lesson ended, but she watched Julie approach Holly and talk to her. She was too far away to hear anything they were saying, but by their faces and body language, it looked like a casual conversation.

"Julie must be keeping it low-key," Leslie muttered to the horse she was riding. He flicked his ears at her in response.

Holly was gone by the time Leslie was done, so she went to find Julie.

"Have any luck?" she asked her when she found her in the feed room.

Julie was measuring supplements for the horses. "Well, I tried to keep it casual so she wouldn't catch on that you said something. I asked her about school, and her boyfriend and how everything was going, and she said everything was great, but I can see what you mean about her looking sad.

"I asked her if she was going to that dance with you, and that you seemed really excited about it. She told me what she told you, that Todd doesn't like dances and doesn't want to do what she wants to do. So, I talked to her about standing up for herself and that relationships should be give and take."

"How did she respond?" Leslie asked anxiously.

"She just kind of shrugged it off. The unfortunate thing about these situations, Leslie, is that the person has to decide for themselves how much to put up with." Julie shrugged and picked up some buckets to carry out the door. "Until you think he's actually hurting her in some way, I think the best thing you can do is be a friend to her and hope she realizes there are better guys out there. If you try too hard to break them up or give your opinion, you might make her mad at you.

"Sorry, Leslie, but that's the best I can offer."

Leslie bit her lip and nodded, knowing Julie was right. "Thanks, Julie. I appreciate the effort."

Leslie walked up to the house to clean up for dinner. While she walked, she wondered if Holly was making a big mistake in dating Todd, or if Leslie was overreacting.

Sundays were everybody's day off at the barn. Helen and Leslie teamed up to feed the horses in the morning, then took showers and climbed into the car to go dress shopping.

"So, Holly's not going with us?" Helen asked while she started the car. "I thought you guys were going to double date."

Helen's question made Leslie realize she had not had time to tell her stepmother about Holly's troubling relationship with Todd, so she explained everything that had happened the day before.

Helen frowned. "I can understand why you're concerned about her, and she did seem kind of down during her lesson yesterday, but I'm afraid Julie's right. Unless we think Holly is in some kind of danger, we just have to trust her to make the decision for herself whether this is the right relationship for her."

"I understand, but it's hard to sit by and do nothing, knowing she's not happy."

"As you grow older, I'm afraid that will happen a lot.

Sometimes people make choices you know are not very good ones, but there's nothing you can do but be supportive and help them do the right thing when the time comes."

Leslie nodded in understanding.

"But let's not dwell on that. We're going shopping for your first formal, and we should be having fun!"

"Yes, let's do that. I'm looking forward to it!" Leslie resolved to put Holly and Todd out of her mind, at least for the day, and concentrated on what kind of dress she might like to buy instead.

When they pulled into the parking lot at the mall a few minutes later, it was packed with cars.

"Why they have to have the Christmas formal in the middle of Christmas shopping season, I don't know. Don't they know how busy the malls are?" Helen grumped good-naturedly.

Leslie giggled. "Um, Mom? It's a Christmas formal. It sort of has to happen during the Christmas season by definition."

Helen heaved an exaggerated sigh. "I guess you're right. A Christmas formal in September would be pretty silly, wouldn't it?"

They finally found a place to park when a car backed out of a space right in front of them, and Helen quickly pulled in.

"We need to make sure we don't leave anything valuable in sight in the car," Helen instructed while they climbed out. "The Christmas season brings out a lot of desperate people, and we don't want anyone to break in."

They checked the front and back seats carefully to make sure there was nothing valuable in the car, then locked the doors and walked across the parking lot to the mall entrance.

"Have you thought about what kind of dress you want to buy?" Helen asked.

"Well, all the girls are wearing long dresses this year, which I like, so I think I'll get a long one. Blue, I think."

"Makes sense, since that's your favorite color."

They consulted the store directory at the entrance to the mall and selected a likely-sounding store. "This sounds like a good one. I've heard some of the other girls talk about getting their dresses there," said Leslie.

They walked through the crowded mall, watching the shoppers hurrying to and fro, laden with shopping bags. Leslie eyed the groups of girls that huddled together, giggling and talking animatedly, and the groups of boys who walked around acting tough.

"I just can't identify with any of them," she told Helen, nodding her head in the other kids' direction. "It's like their whole life is centered on how cool they look."

She shook her head. Although she was not popular in school, she was happy with her life.

"I know what you mean," Helen answered. "I felt the same way about the kids I went to school with. I think this is it." She stopped in front of a store that had several formal dresses hanging in the windows.

"Pretty good bet," Leslie said, smiling.

They walked inside together. The store was crowded with girls from Leslie's high school, all shopping for their Christmas formal dresses. Leslie headed for the sale racks first out of habit, and she was flipping through the selections in her size when Helen tapped her on the shoulder.

Leslie turned to look, and Helen held a floor length, dark blue dress. The bodice was velvet and cut like a halter top with three crystal buttons that ran down the front, and the skirt was a shimmery organza that rustled when it moved. A layer of stiff tulle underneath gave the skirt body.

"It's beautiful!" Leslie gasped.

"I think so too," Helen said, eyes shining. "Why don't you try it on?"

Leslie took the dress and made her way to the back of the store where the dressing rooms were, Helen close behind her.

"Would you like to try that on?" a sales woman asked brightly.

"Yes, please," Leslie answered.

The sales lady looked around and gestured toward a dressing room another girl had just exited.

"Right this way, dear. Just one item?" Leslie nodded, and the woman handed her a card with the number one on it. "Just hang this on your door and give it to me when you're finished."

Leslie stepped into the cramped dressing room and closed the door behind her. She stripped and pulled the dress on over her head. She struggled to pull up the zipper on the side of the bodice, then stepped back as far as she could to look at herself in the mirror.

The person she saw there was not the one she was used to seeing. This one was grown-up looking, with curves where she never noticed having them before. She piled her thick hair on top of her head and tried to imagine what she would look like with makeup and jewelry on.

I could get used to this, she thought, smiling at her reflection.

"Does it fit? How does it look?" Helen's voice floated in from outside of the dressing room. Leslie opened the door in answer and stood for inspection.

"Oh, Leslie. You look gorgeous! Come out here and look in the three-way mirror."

Helen took Leslie's wrist and led her over to a corner where three mirrors stood at an angle to each other. When Leslie stood in the middle, she could see almost every angle of herself. She stood there and admired her reflection for a moment, turning back and forth to get the full effect, savoring how she looked.

"That looks lovely on you, dear." The saleslady had appeared next to Helen, and both of them were beaming as much as Leslie was. "It looks like it fits you perfectly."

"It feels great," Leslie said. "I love it!"

Her eyes sparkled; she had never worn anything like it before.

Another voice said, "Blue looks nice on you, Leslie. You almost don't look poor in that dress."

Leslie saw in the mirror that Kate had appeared next to the saleslady and was watching Leslie with her usual snobby look. Her governess stood behind her.

I've just about had enough of that little brat, Leslie thought, then turned around to look Kate in the eye.

"First of all, Kate, I'm really not that poor, not that I care what you think. At least my mother cared enough to come shopping with me, instead of paying someone else to do it. Shouldn't you be off tending to your flying monkeys or something?"

Kate's mouth fell open, and she stared at Leslie with narrowed eyes for a few seconds. Leslie's heart pounded and blood roared in her ears, but she crossed her arms to keep her hands from shaking and stared coolly back at her rival. Seemingly unable to find anything to say in retort, Kate abruptly snapped her mouth closed, whirled around, and stalked out of the store with her attendant in tow. She was followed by a round of applause from several of the girls who were close enough to hear the exchange.

"I'm sure glad you told her off," one of them said to Leslie. "She thinks she's all that, but she's really just a witch. I think even her friends don't like her very much."

Leslie blushed, not knowing quite how to react. She had not known anyone was listening, and she had just spoken without thinking. Even Helen and the sales lady were trying to cover the fact that they were snickering. Not knowing what to say, Leslie smiled and bowed exaggeratedly, like she was on stage. The girls laughed and turned back to their shopping, chattering excitedly.

Leslie turned to Helen and the saleslady. "I guess that wasn't very ladylike, but she makes me so mad!"

Helen gave up on covering her reaction and said, "I think it was perfect. Flying monkeys!"

She chuckled again.

"So, do you think you would like that one, dear, or would you like to try something else?" the sales woman asked.

"Oh!" Leslie said, almost forgetting what she was doing there. She looked down at the price tag that hung from the side seam of the dress, and her expression changed from delight to sorrow.

"Oh. I'm sorry, this is much more than I can spend."

Helen stepped forward and put her hand on Leslie's arm.

"Leslie, don't be silly. I'll buy this for you, and I don't want to hear another word about it."

Leslie's eyes filled with tears and she gave Helen a fierce hug. "Oh, Mom! Thank you! It's absolutely gorgeous, and I love it!"

The sales woman pulled off the tag and walked with Helen to the register to pay, and Leslie went back into the dressing room to change, loving the feel of the skirt swirling around her feet. Although she walked, she felt more like she floated. After she changed, the sales woman wrapped the dress in a pink bag and handed the hanger to Leslie, who carried it out of the store as though it were precious treasure.

"Having a good day so far, Leslie?" Helen asked once they exited the shop.

"I think this ranks right up there as one of the best days of my life!" Leslie answered.

"Well, how about we go get some accessories to wear with this dress, and then we can get some lunch?"

The rest of the day passed pleasantly, with no more encounters with Kate. Leslie found a rhinestone earring and necklace set she liked with dark blue stones to match the dress. After Helen and Leslie shared lunch at the mall, they started back for home together. While Helen drove, Leslie called Holly on her cell phone to tell her all about her shopping trip.

When Leslie relayed the part about the confrontation with Kate, Holly broke out into a laughing fit and could not stop for a couple of minutes.

While Leslie waited for her friend to regain control, she thought, *Now* this *is the Holly I know!*

Finally, Holly managed to stop laughing. "That's the best news I've heard in a while, Leslie. Good for you! So, do you want some help getting ready for the dance? I could come over for a while before I go on my date with Todd."

"Are you sure? I would love it, but not if it will put

you out too much."

"I'd love to. Since I can't go to the dance, I can at least enjoy it a little through you. Would four o'clock be OK?"

"That would be perfect."

Chapter Ten:
The Dance

Leslie lay on her back on the bed staring at the ceiling. She had about thirty minutes before Holly would arrive, and she had already taken her shower and dried her hair. She had all of her hair and makeup stuff set out, along with her dress and the jewelry she'd bought to go with it. She had just applied some deep red fingernail polish, and she didn't want to move or touch anything for fear she would smudge it. Afraid to even pick up a book or magazine, all she could do was stare at the ceiling and wrestle with her own thoughts.

Primarily, her thoughts surrounded her dilemma about Holly. No one else seemed concerned about how Todd treated her, including Holly, but Leslie knew something wasn't right. A scene from lunchtime the day before ran through her mind, when Holly had been talking to her science lab partner about their project. Austin had said something funny, and Holly laughed in response.

Todd walked into the cafeteria at that moment, and Leslie watched while he stomped across the room and pointed at them both like he was lecturing them. He then grabbed Holly by the arm and practically dragged her out of the room. They argued the whole way.

Leslie had sat across the room and watched the whole thing in shock. It was all over before she could think or react, not that she would have known what to do if she had the opportunity. She didn't have a chance to talk to Holly for the rest of the day to ask her what it was all about. While she lay there, staring at the ceiling, she wondered if it was time to talk to Holly about her boyfriend.

She checked out the paint job on her fingers and sighed. "Why can I never get them perfect?" she asked herself aloud. "They're always all squiggly and I get polish all over my fingers. Holly's always look perfect."

Satisfied that her fingernails were dry enough to move, she rolled over and looked at the clock. It was ten after four, and Holly should have been there already.

Not like her to be late, she thought. *Guess I can start getting dressed.*

She stood and changed into her dress, but Holly still hadn't arrived. She put on her makeup, trying to remember all the tips she'd learned from Holly and Helen since she started wearing it. She had to start over a couple of times to make sure it was right, but she finally decided she was satisfied. She was just getting ready to tackle her hair when Holly let herself into the room. Leslie looked over at the clock that read four forty-five. She raised an eyebrow and looked up at her friend.

"I know I'm late, and I'm sorry," Holly started. "Todd and I had a big fight."

Leslie tried to keep her annoyance in check and feel

some sympathy for her friend, but it was a struggle.

"What about?" she asked, carefully controlling the tone of her voice.

Holly flopped on the bed and sighed. Averting her eyes, she said, "He didn't want me coming over here to help you. He thinks we spend too much time together."

Leslie dropped the brush she was holding for her hair.

"What? Are you serious?"

The corners of Holly's mouth turned down in a frown and tears welled up in her eyes. She opened her mouth to respond, but then closed it again and nodded. She continued to stare at the floor.

Leslie's mouth fell open, and it took her a minute to respond. "How can he say that? I've hardly seen you since you two got together."

Holly shrugged. "Well, he says it's too much. He said I should be home making myself pretty for him instead of wasting my time with you."

Leslie didn't know how to react. What Holly said was so ridiculous she could hardly believe her ears. "Well, what are you supposed to do, never come to the barn, either?"

Holly shrugged, still refusing to meet Leslie's eyes.

"He says I need to grow up and learn how to be a good girlfriend, not spend so much time with the horses like a little girl."

"Holly, you can't be serious. You aren't really going to give in to this, are you? I mean, he's being a complete jerk!"

Before Leslie's eyes, a change came over her friend. Holly sat up straight, crossed her arms, and looked Leslie coldly in the eye.

"I don't appreciate your calling my boyfriend names. He and I may have our problems, but we can work it out." She stood up and put her hands on her hips and added, "Not all of us can be perfect like you and Alex, so I'll thank you to keep your opinions to yourself."

With that, she flounced out, slamming the door behind her. Leslie didn't move for a minute, staring open-mouthed after her friend. After a minute, shock turned to anger.

I can't believe she's taking his side over mine! She thought, furious, while she ran the brush through her hair. *How can she not see what a jerk he is? She's known me forever — and him for just a few months — and she's going to listen to him telling her not to spend time with me? Or her horse?*

Hardly knowing what to do with her hair and angry all over again with Holly for promising to help and then flaking, Leslie struggled with putting her hair up. She rarely did anything with it other than putting it in a pony tail, and she had been relying on Holly's expertise to do something elegant with it.

She was fighting back tears when her bedroom door opened and Helen stuck her head in. "Holly just ran out the door. Is everything OK?"

Leslie opened her mouth to tell her stepmother what happened, but burst into tears instead. Helen rushed to her side and wrapped her arms around Leslie's shoulders, holding her and rocking her from side to side.

"Sshh, it'll be OK, whatever it is. You're going to smear your makeup that you did such a lovely job on."

After a couple of sharp intakes of breath, Leslie managed to get herself under control enough to tell Helen what had happened between her and Holly, including what she had seen in the lunch room the day before. Helen just held her and listened.

She finished with, "So I guess you and Julie were right. I should have just kept my mouth shut. I just thought he'd gone too far this time, and I couldn't stand to see her so sad."

"Well, honey, I can't say I blame you. You know Holly better than just about anyone, and if you think she's unhappy, there's probably something to that. I have to say I'm a little concerned that he's telling her not to spend so much time around you and her horse. Isolating her from her friends is classic behavior for an abuser. Would you like me to have a talk with her mother?"

Leslie shook her head.

"She's already mad at me for even saying anything, and she probably doesn't even want to be friends anymore." The words brought on a fresh batch of tears.

"Now, don't go rushing to conclusions. Holly's upset and confused right now, but that doesn't mean she doesn't want to be friends anymore. Just be patient, and she'll come around again; you'll see. Tell you what: If you see anything else from Todd that you think puts Holly in danger or is making her really miserable, tell me and I'll either talk to her or her mother, OK? She might be willing to listen to an adult."

Leslie sniffed and nodded, taking a tissue off her vanity to wipe her tears.

"OK, I guess that seems fair. Thanks, Mom. Now, I guess I have to try to get ready without her. I don't see how I'm going to enjoy the dance now, but I can't disappoint Alex. Will you help me?"

"Of course! Here, let's start by getting rid of that runny mascara."

With Helen's help, Leslie was ready in no time, and they were putting on the finishing touches when Dan knocked softly on the door to tell them Alex and his parents were downstairs. Leslie automatically wiped her sweaty palms on the skirt of her dress, then she cringed and quickly grabbed a tissue to make sure she hadn't left a damp spot.

Helen laughed. "You aren't nervous, are you? You and Alex have been dating for months."

Leslie's mouth felt dry. "I know, but this is different! This is a dance, and dinner, and we're all dressed up, and... and..."

"And you'll be fine. And it'll be fun. And you'll be glad you went, and then you can tell me all about it when you get home." Helen put her arm around Leslie's shoulder while she spoke. "Now let's go downstairs and rescue Alex from your father. How much do you want to bet Alex is just as nervous as you are, and Dan is just making it worse by teasing him?"

Leslie couldn't help but smile at that, and she felt a little more at ease. She nodded and allowed Helen to lead her out of the room. Her stepmother stopped her at the top of the stairs.

"Wait here. You need to make a grand entrance, so let me get down there first and get the camera ready."

Leslie giggled and waited until she heard Helen announce her grandly, like she were some kind of princess arriving at a ball. As she descended the stairs, her heart lightened and her smile grew. She forgot all about her fight with Holly while she enjoyed the attention from her family and boyfriend, who all stood in the living room and watched her walk down the stairs. She held onto the banister for support, praying silently that she wouldn't trip and fall on her way down, especially since Helen and Alex's mother, Cecilia, kept taking pictures and blinding her with the flash.

"OK, you two. Enough!" she said with a laugh when she got to the bottom of the stairs. "I'm seeing spots!"

She was able to see enough to notice her father and Alex's father Mark jabbing a wide-eyed Alex in the ribs with their elbows. Alex jumped, blinked, closed his mouth and cleared his throat before stepping forward and handing her a plastic box.

"Um, I got you this," he said haltingly, then blushed.

Leslie smiled; Helen had been right. She opened the box to find a corsage made from a large lily. The petals were creamy, but had a purple blush that started at the center of the flower and worked its way out to the tips.

Leslie drank in the fragrance before saying, "Alex, it's lovely! I love stargazers. How did you know?"

Alex's cheeks turned a little darker shade of red, and his eyes looked everywhere but at hers. "Oh, I asked around."

Leslie glanced up at the adults and saw them all looking at each other and smiling, so she figured they might have had something to do with it. She started to take the corsage out of the box, but Alex took it from her.

"Uh, allow me."

He fumbled it out of the box, dropped it, picked it up, and clumsily shoved the wristband over her wrist, then smiled proudly at his accomplishment.

"I love it, Alex. Thank you," Leslie said, laying a hand gently on his arm. She leaned over and kissed him on his crimson cheek, and the room lit up with twin flashes again. Luckily, Leslie's eyes were shielded that time by Alex's face, and she was spared from yet another light spot dancing around on her vision. She could feel Alex take a big breath and relax just a little.

"Well, I guess we should get going," she said, glancing toward the door.

"Oh, no you don't!" Helen said, blocking the way. She held up the camera and waggled it.

"Did you really think we'd let you get all dressed up without taking hundreds of pictures of you?" Cecilia added, her free hand planted firmly on her hip. "Into the living room, you two. We have plenty of time to embarrass you before your dinner reservation."

Alex rolled his eyes, and Leslie could see that his cheeks had returned to his normal color and his nervousness seemed to have passed. He pulled himself up straight, put his chin in the air and held his arm out to her.

"M'lady, shall I escort you to the living room for embarrassment?"

Leslie slipped her hand into the crook of his arm. "You shall, M'lord!"

They trooped into the living room with the adults following along behind. Leslie stood dutifully in front of the fireplace with Alex and let Helen and Cecilia take pictures to their hearts' content. Alex fidgeted beside her in embarrassment, but Leslie had learned to just let the adults have their way when it came to taking pictures. It was inevitable, so there was no use fighting it.

"I think we've tortured them sufficiently, don't you?" Helen finally said to Cecilia, who appeared to think about it for a moment before nodding her agreement.

"Can we *go* now? We need time to get to the restaurant, and we don't want to miss our reservation," Alex said.

"Come on, dear, time to let the kids have their night," Mark said. "If you keep this up, you'll scar them for life." Leslie smiled at him in gratitude. She had only met him a couple of times, but she really liked him. His words made her like him even more.

There was little conversation on the way to the restaurant, where Mark and Cecilia would also be eating so they could take the kids to the dance afterward. They had promised to request a table far away from Alex and Leslie so they could all have some privacy for their date.

The restaurant was an Italian place Leslie had never been to but had always wanted to try. It was in an old Victorian style house with a lot of small rooms, so once the hostess seated them at a cozy table by a window, she felt as though she had Alex all to herself. There were only three other tables in the room, each occupied by quiet couples who gazed romantically at each other and spoke in low tones.

Leslie picked up her menu and scanned the choices.

"Everything looks so good; I don't know what to have."

She saw several dishes she thought she would like, but she felt self conscious about ordering something too expensive. She knew Alex's family didn't have a lot of money, and she didn't know how much he would have to spend.

She glanced up to see that Alex was studying his own menu, biting his lip while he read.

"Some of this stuff looks so fancy. Don't they just have plain old spaghetti and meatballs?"

Leslie giggled. "On the back, down at the bottom."

Alex looked where she told him and looked up at her with narrowed eyes.

"The kids menu? Very funny, Ms. Clark." He smiled and shook his head and continued reading, then pointed to a section on the third page. "Here it is."

Leslie found the page in her own menu. She was relieved to see that the price was lower than many of the other items on the menu.

"Oh, that looks good," she said as casually as she could. "I'm going to have that, too."

They chatted easily about school and horses throughout the meal, and Leslie tried not to let her eyes bug out when Alex asked for a third basket of bread. She was full halfway through her entrée and just one of the delicious sourdough rolls.

She instinctively answered "No, thank you," when the waitress asked if they wanted dessert, but the woman was too busy writing down Alex's louder order of two slices of the restaurant's specialty cheesecake. She sighed and resigned herself to the fact that she was going to be uncomfortably full all evening.

It didn't take long for the cheesecake to arrive.

I hope I don't pop a seam on this dress! she thought while she picked up her fork to dig in.

When Alex finished his last bite, he sat back and patted his stomach.

"That wasn't bad. The portions were kind of small, but I guess I got enough to eat."

Leslie shook her head and laughed. "You're like a human vacuum cleaner. I've never seen anyone who could eat so much and still be so skinny."

Alex winked. "It's my secret weapon."

He paid the check, and they went outside to see his parents when they had just made it to the car.

"Good timing!" Leslie said when they climbed in.

The ride to the school was short, but Leslie put the time to good use, worrying about whether she would make a fool of herself at the dance. *What if everyone notices I don't know how to dance and laughs at me? Kate will for sure. Why did I ever agree to this?*

She slid a glance across the backseat, and she saw a rivulet of sweat running down the side of Alex's face. He clasped and unclasped his hands, then wiped his palms on his pants.

He's as nervous as I am, even though this was all his idea!

She smiled, remembering how nervous they both had been on their first date before they realized they both felt the same way and started to have fun. She didn't expect to feel that nervous again, but even though she was with the same boy, it was a whole new experience going to a formal dance.

When they pulled up at the school, Alex told her to stay put. She waited while he exited the car and ran around to her side to open her door and help her out, and out of the corner of her eye she saw Mark winking at his wife. She waved goodbye to them, Alex closed the car door, and then they turned together to face the school and their classmates, who were all heading inside. Couples walked arm-in-arm, laughing and talking.

Leslie took a deep breath and let it out, and she felt Alex doing the same beside her. She turned to look at him and saw her insecurity reflected in his eyes, so she mustered up a smile.

"Let's go have some fun," she said, and she thought she made it sound pretty convincing. He smiled back at her, she took his arm and they went inside together.

"It's beautiful!" she exclaimed when they walked through the door and she saw how the gym was decorated.

She saw Alex nod out of the corner of her eye.

"Those silver streamers are pretty. They make it look like it's raining or snowing or something." He had to shout so she could hear her over the blasting music.

"I like the centerpieces," she shouted back, pointing to the arrangements of blue, silver and white flowers that sat on small tables around the edge of the room. The white linen table cloths added an elegant look, and Leslie almost forgot that she stood in her high school gymnasium instead of a fancy banquet hall. There were even white trees scattered around that sparkled with silver leaves and white twinkle lights.

The dance floor was already filled with kids dancing, arms wrapped around each other and slowly swaying to the love song that filled the air. Alex grabbed her hand and dragged her out to the middle of the pack. She started to protest, but it seemed he couldn't hear her over the music. She shrugged and allowed herself to be dragged along.

When he finally stopped, he leaned over and said in her ear, "It's a slow one. I think I can handle this."

He looked around, and then put his hands on her hips. She put her hands on his shoulders like she'd seen a lot of the other girls do, and they shuffled to the music together. Leslie had seen some of the other kids holding each other more closely, but she wasn't ready to squish herself up against Alex like that, especially in public. She could feel her cheeks heating up, and she hoped the room was dark enough he couldn't see. The disco ball and colored lights made enough light to see shapes, but it was hard to see details.

When the song ended, a faster one came on and Leslie

and Alex broke apart to fast dance. Leslie tried to remember the little bit she'd learned in gym class but felt silly doing it. She noticed Alex didn't seem to be doing much better, and neither were a lot of the kids around them, so she decided not to worry about it and just have fun.

After two dances, Leslie was soaked in sweat. She leaned over to Alex and said, "I think I need a break!"

"Cake?" Alex asked, furrowing his brow. "I thought you were full!"

Leslie laughed and shook her head. She moved her mouth closer to Alex's ear and shouted, "Not cake! Break! I need a break!"

Alex's forehead smoothed over and he nodded. "Oh! Yeah, me too."

He took her hand and led her through the writhing mass of kids until they were off the dance floor. Leslie was jostled several times and almost lost his hand and got separated, but she managed to hang on.

"I need to use the bathroom," she told him once she thought he could hear her.

"What? Your dress is an heirloom? It's pretty!"

Leslie gave an exasperated sigh. "Not heirloom! Bathroom! I need to use the bathroom!"

He nodded again in understanding. "Oh! Right. Come on, I'll wait for you in the hallway."

He led her to the hall where the bathrooms were and promised to wait right outside for her. She pushed her way through the door, and Kate bumped into her on the way out.

"Watch it, charity case," the girl snarled, and her friends tittered and cast mocking glances Leslie's way as they pushed past her. She rolled her eyes and willed the heat to leave her cheeks, but she was still hot from dancing.

Once she was all the way into the bathroom, she felt a deliciously cold blast of air from the open windows. She sighed in relief and stood there for a minute, cooling down, before she let herself into a stall. She was relieved no one else was in the room to witness what Kate had said to her. Plus, it was nice to be alone for a few minutes after the press of the crowded dance floor.

By the time she finished using the toilet and had washed and dried her hands, the room was filled with girls again. They giggled and whispered to each other, looking at her from time to time. It was something she was used to ever since she had known Kate, but it wasn't as easy to shrug it off as she thought it should be. She took a deep breath and squared her shoulders, refusing to look at the giggling girls. She looked herself over to make sure she didn't have toilet paper hanging off her dress or something, determined they were just being nasty, and marched to the door to leave.

She immediately moved from a bright, cool world to a dark, hot and noisy one. However, that was not what stopped her in her tracks before she'd gone more than two steps from the bathroom door.

It was the sight of Alex kissing Kate that stopped her in her tracks.

Chapter Eleven:
Resolution

Leslie lay on her bed, staring at the ceiling. She felt raw and empty inside, empty even of tears after crying for several hours. As she lay there, she thought of the irony of the fact that she had lain in that exact same spot just a few hours before, waiting for Holly to get there to help her get ready. Then, everything had changed. Her boyfriend had kissed her most hated enemy, and she couldn't even talk to her best friend about it, because Holly was mad at her.

"What am I going to do?" she asked her ceiling, but it didn't answer.

While she stared at the white plaster, the scene at the dance ran through her mind over and over. She had stepped out of the bathroom to see Kate's arms around Alex's neck and her lips pressed to his. She didn't even stop to confront them, just burst into tears and pushed her way through the crowd in the hallway and across the main room of the gym. She had faintly heard Alex calling her name, but she refused to stop or turn around. She vaguely remembered talking a teacher into driving her home, and that she'd had to convince her father and Helen that she really didn't want to talk about it.

She had been home for hours, but she hadn't gathered up the energy even to take her dress off and get ready for bed. She had been too busy crying at first, and then she just lay there, motionless. Finally, her eyes drooped and she decided she might as well go to bed. She dragged herself upright and changed into pajamas. She wanted to throw the dress, her first real formal, out the window and forget the night had ever happened. At the last moment, she thought of how much Helen had paid for it and changed her mind. She hung it neatly in the back of her closet and put the jewelry in a box on the shelf above.

The next morning, she opened her eyes to see Helen sitting on the edge of her bed. Leslie stared dully at her stepmother.

"I still don't want to talk about it," she said, then pulled the blanket over her head and rolled over to go back to sleep.

Leslie felt Helen's hand on her knee. "Honey, I don't know what's going on, but Alex is downstairs and he's really upset. Why don't you come down and talk to him?"

"No way. He did the worst thing anyone could ever do. I'll never forgive him, and I'm never talking to him again. I don't even want him at the barn anymore."

"Now, Leslie. Alex is my employee, so you don't get to fire him. You at least owe me an explanation of what happened."

Leslie pushed the blanket down and stared at her. "But that's not fair! I'm your daughter!"

"Well, I'm perfectly willing to discuss it," Helen said, crossing her arms. "The Alex I know is a fine, upstanding young man who opens the door for you and tells everyone who will listen how lucky he is to have you as a girl-friend. I can't imagine him doing anything as awful as you say."

"Well, he did, and I'll never forgive him."

"You mentioned that." Helen's tone softened, and she took Leslie's hand. "Now, won't you tell me what happened last night?"

Leslie heaved a sigh and rolled her eyes up toward the ceiling.

"He kissed Kate!" she blurted out just before she burst into tears. She had thought she had run out, but sleeping seemed to have refilled her supply.

Helen gathered her up, hugged her and rocked her back and forth. "Sshh, it can't be true. Alex loves you too much for that. He hates Kate almost as much as you do."

"I saw him!" Leslie managed between sobs. "They were right there in front of everyone."

Helen was silent for a moment, but she continued her squeezing and rocking. When she spoke, her voice was soothing. "I believe you saw what you say you did, but surely there must be some explanation. That just doesn't sound like Alex, and he's downstairs begging to talk to you. He's really upset, Les. Won't you please at least come hear him out?"

Leslie sighed and thought it over for a minute until she got her tears under control. Finally, she said, "I guess I might as well get some closure. Just give me a few minutes to clean up and get dressed. I'm sure I look awful. I don't want him to see me like this."

When Leslie went downstairs twenty minutes later, she was showered, dressed and all traces of the smeared makeup from the night before had been removed. She couldn't do anything about her puffy, red eyes, however, despite splashing them with cold water. She found Alex in the kitchen eating pancakes, but he put his fork down as soon as she walked in. Dan was setting another plate of them on the table.

"Here you go, honey," he said, pulling out the chair for her. "You might as well eat while you talk."

Leslie had no appetite, and she couldn't understand how Alex could be shoveling pancakes in his mouth at such a time. However, she had to admit to herself that he did look upset. She stared at her plate and waited for him to speak, not trusting her own voice.

Alex picked up his fork and poked at his pancakes. "It wasn't what it looked like, Leslie. You have to believe me."

"I'm not sure how I could possibly misinterpret what I saw. That horrible Kate was wrapped around you, and you were kissing each other."

Leslie felt like she might throw up.

Alex dropped the fork on the plate and grabbed her hand in both of his. She curled her lip; they were sticky with pancake syrup. "Leslie, I swear. I hate her. You know that. Why would I kiss her?"

Leslie slowly closed her eyes and opened them again, then finally met his gaze. "Then why were you?"

"I was standing there in the hallway waiting for you, and Kate came out of the bathroom with all her snotty friends. They all stood there talking for a minute, giggling and looking at me, and I tried to ignore them. Kate came over and said I looked handsome in my tux, and I didn't know what to do, so I just said, "Thanks."

"The next thing I know, she's wrapping her arms around me and kissing me. I was so shocked I just froze for a second, and I was just getting ready to push her away when you came out and saw us. I swear, that's the truth."

Leslie sighed and took her hand back. "Why should I believe you? Kate is beautiful. I'm sure any boy would want to kiss her."

She tried to wipe the sticky stuff off her hands with a napkin, but it wouldn't budge.

Alex tried again, his tone pleading. "Think about it, Leslie. Why would I want to kiss someone I hate, when I love you so much? Besides, you were right on the other side of the door. Kate is always trying to hurt you, and she knew this was just about the worst thing she could do to you."

Leslie thought it over, and she had to admit to herself that he had a point. Her heart lifted a little, but she hardly dared to hope he was telling the truth. She lifted her gaze to his again. The misery she saw there made her heart lift a little more, but she needed just a little more reassurance.

"Alex, do you swear this is true?"

He looked at her sincerely and steadily, and his tone was very serious. "I swear, Leslie. I would never, ever hurt you like that. You mean the world to me."

"And you hate Kate?"

"More than anything."

Leslie could see a glimmer of hope in his eyes, and she knew he was telling the truth. She threw her arms around him and buried her face in his neck.

"I'm so sorry, Alex. I should have known better. That Kate is just awful, and I should have known you'd never kiss her on purpose."

Alex held her close. "No, you had a right to be mad, Leslie. I should have pushed her away faster. I shouldn't have let her get to me at all."

"Now that you're both sorry, will you please eat your pancakes so all my hard work doesn't go to waste?"

Leslie released her hold and laughed up at her father. "Dad!"

He pointed meaningfully at her plate and raised an eyebrow, and she dutifully picked up her fork and started in on her breakfast. Alex was already way ahead of her.

In the following weeks, Leslie avoided Holly as much as she could, and her former best friend did the same. Leslie made sure she was busy whenever Holly was at the barn, which was much less frequent than it had been before Holly started dating Todd.

"Are you two ever going to speak to each other again?" Alex asked Leslie one day.

Leslie shrugged. "It's up to her. She's the one who's mad at me. She's the one who stormed out after promising to help me, remember?"

"Well, maybe you should just apologize. I mean, you two have been friends forever."

"Are you kidding? I'm not apologizing for anything. I didn't do anything wrong. Now, come on. I need to work this horse."

She had the same conversation with her father, with Helen and with Julie. They all tried to convince her that she should approach Holly and put an end to the fight. She refused every time.

"I didn't do anything wrong," she maintained.

The last Saturday before Christmas break was over,

Leslie was reading the training board to see her assignments for the day when Helen came out of the office.

"Holly cancelled her lesson again. You can ride Sundance for her," she said, writing Leslie's initials next to Holly's horse's name.

Leslie felt an instant pang of resentment. "Why do I have to do it? We're not speaking, remember?"

"Mostly because I said so. I'm your boss and your mother, remember?"

"But—"

"But nothing. You know I have too many lessons today to be able to ride. You like riding Sundance, so it's not like I'm asking you for some big sacrifice. I'm sorry you're fighting with Holly, but you're just going to have to be a professional and do your job."

Leslie was stricken by her stepmother's words and tone. Helen was usually kind and rarely spoke so harshly to her. Tears of anger and frustration welled up in her eyes, and she turned and stomped away before Helen could see them.

Sundance was lying down when she got to his stall. "Come on, boy, time to get up and go to work," she told him while she unbuckled his halter from the bar on the door. "You can finish your nap later."

He groaned, and she giggled, her frustration forgotten. She thought he probably sounded a lot like she did when someone woke her up earlier than she wanted. She let herself into the stall and slipped the halter over the gelding's head, but he still refused to get up. He was lying on his belly with his legs curled up next to him and his muzzle resting lazily in the shavings. He turned his head to bite at his belly, although it was too cold for flies.

"Come on, Sundance. I don't have all day," she informed him, using the lead rope to pull his head toward his tail. She hoped to make him uncomfortable enough he would get up. Instead, he groaned again, closed his eyes and lay down flat on his side, pulling the lead rope through her fingers. He kicked at his stomach with his hind leg.

The situation lost its charm, and Leslie felt the frustration returning. "OK, seriously. Come *on*."

She bent down by his head and noticed for the first time that the delicate skin above his nostrils was wrinkled, which often signals that a horse is in pain. She used her thumb to lift his eyelid, and his eye looked glazed. Her heart felt like a fist had closed around it, and her stomach lurched in fear.

"Sundance, are you colicking?"

Leslie knew that colic was one of the scariest things to happen to a horse. It could be as mild as a stomachache or severe enough that the horse could need surgery or even die.

"Helen!" She shouted, stroking the horse on the neck. "Julie! Alex! Anybody!"

A moment later, they all appeared in the doorway within seconds of each other.

"What's going on?" Helen asked. "What's the matter?"

The tears of frustration Leslie had fought back just a few minutes before became tears of panic. They welled up and spilled down her cheeks as she spoke. "I think Sundance is colicking. He won't get up, he's biting and kicking at his belly even though there aren't any flies, and I think he's in pain."

"Alex, go get the thermometer, a syringe and the bottle of Banamine from the med drawer in the tack room. Julie, go call Dr. Burke." Helen spoke crisply and calmly, but Leslie could see worry lines forming around her eyes.

The other two sprang into action, and Helen walked into the stall.

"This definitely looks like colic to me. I'm glad you came to get him first, or someone might not have noticed until it was too late. Here, help me get him up. We have to keep him from rolling, or he could twist his intestine. If he does that, he could die."

Leslie pulled on the lead rope again, pulling Sundance's head toward his feet while Helen pushed on his back from the other side. He weighed three times what the two of them did put together, so they couldn't force him. They kept pushing and pulling, and after a minute or so he slowly responded. He rolled up onto his belly, and then paused, breathing heavily. Leslie and Helen stopped their efforts to let him rest.

"That's it, boy! You can do it!" Leslie said, bending down to stroke his neck. The hair behind his ears had darkened with sweat.

"OK, let's get him up the rest of the way," Helen said

after a minute had passed.

Leslie resumed her pulling while Helen pushed, and finally Sundance made a big effort and dragged himself to his feet. Leslie let out a cry of relief.

"Is he going to be OK? Is he going to die?"

"It's too soon to say, Leslie. We really need to let the vet look at him before we'll know anything."`

Julie came in holding her cell phone to her ear.

"Right. OK. Here she is."

She handed the phone to Helen.

Leslie was barely aware of the conversation Helen was having on the phone. She was focused on Sundance, holding his head in her arms and cradling it to her chest while she stroked his neck and murmured soothing words to him. Even though he was Holly's horse, Leslie felt like she loved him almost as much as she did Lucky. She immediately felt guilty, realizing that she hadn't even visited Lucky in weeks.

At the thought of Holly, Leslie's eyes popped wide open. "I have to call Holly!"

She let go of Sundance's head and fished her cell phone out of her pocket. She held down the two button and listened to the tones of the speed dial.

"Pick up, pick up, pick up!" she said, but the call went to voice mail mid-way through the second ring. It wasn't until then that she remembered Holly wasn't talking to her. She figured her name must have shown up on Holly's caller ID. She hung up in frustration, knowing Holly wouldn't even listen to her message if she left a voicemail.

Helen was still talking to the vet, looking at Sundance's gums and describing the color into the phone. Leslie bit her lip, wondering what she should do. She looked around the stall and saw that Alex was still standing there, looking worried.

She handed him the lead rope she held. "Here, hold Sundance. I've got to find a way to get a hold of Holly."

He opened his mouth to respond, but she didn't wait to hear. She ran out of the stall and down the barn aisle to the office to use the phone there. She hoped if Holly's Caller ID showed that Green Meadow was calling instead of Leslie, she would answer.

Holly's line rang three times, and then a familiar male voice answered.

"Hello?" When Leslie was too surprised to say anything for a moment, he repeated himself. "Hello? Is anyone there?"

"T-Todd? This is Leslie. I really need to talk to Holly. It's an emergency. Sundance—"

"Listen to me," he interrupted, his words slow and measured. His hostility carried through the line loud and clear. "Stop bothering Holly. I've had enough of you trying to come between us."

The line clicked, and he was gone. Leslie growled and cast about for another idea. "Who can I have call her so she'll answer?" she mused aloud.

She chewed her thumbnail while she thought, then picked up the phone and dialed again.

This time, she called Holly's house.

"Please be home," she murmured.

She was rewarded a moment later when Mrs. Moore answered. Leslie quickly explained the whole situation, and Holly's mother promised to track Holly down and get her to the barn. Leslie sighed with relief and ran back down the aisle to Sundance's stall.

Helen was wearing a stethoscope and holding the end of it to various places on Sundance's belly.

"What is she doing?" Leslie asked Alex.

"Dr. Burke told her to listen for gut sounds."

Helen took off the stethoscope and put it around her neck. She then took Julie's cell phone from her and spoke into it. "I don't hear anything."

She listened for a moment, nodding and looking around the stall.

"Right. There's no manure in here, so I don't think he's passed anything for a while... Yep, I think you're right... OK, see you soon."

She hung up and handed the phone back to Julie. Her eyes were creased with worry.

"She said it sounds like an impaction colic, which means that something is stuck in his intestine. She told me to give him some Banamine for the pain, and she wants us to give him some mineral oil and probiotics to see if we can get his bowel moving. Julie, do you know where it is?"

The assistant trainer nodded and ran out of the stall. Helen turned back to Leslie and Alex. "Dr. Burke will be by in an hour or so to check on him, but if he gets any worse we need to call her. I guess I'd better go call Holly."

"I already did," Leslie said, feeling miserable. Helen looked at her, eyebrows raised in surprise. Leslie's eyes dropped to the floor, and she explained everything that had happened when she tried to get a hold of her friend.

"Well, that was very mature of you, Leslie. Thank you for going through all that, even though you and Holly aren't speaking."

Leslie looked at her stepmother again. "How could I not? This is Sundance we're talking about here. He could die!"

She burst into tears, and Alex and Helen both stepped

closer and enveloped her in a group hug.

"Shh, it'll be all right, Leslie. Sundance should be fine. He's not thrashing around like a horse in a lot of pain, so it can't be that bad. We'll do everything we can to help him."

Julie came back, and Helen gave Sundance a healthy dose of mineral oil and probiotics by squirting them into his mouth. "This should help his bowels move. Leslie, why don't you see if you can get him to drink? Dr. Burke said to take him for a little walk for about twenty minutes every hour, then let him rest. Maybe you and Alex can take turns babysitting him until Holly gets here. Do you think you can handle that so I can go teach?"

Leslie nodded, and the trainer left, followed by Julie.

"Go ahead and go do your chores, Alex. I'll take the first shift with Sundance." Alex gave her a hug and then went on his way, and Leslie led Sundance out of the stall.

"I guess it's just you and me, boy."

She walked Sundance around the indoor arena for a while, then took him back to his stall. She sat with her back to the wall and thought about Holly and Todd while she watched Sundance wander around listlessly. From time to time, she tried to get him to drink from the automatic waterer in the corner, but he refused.

After an hour, Alex came in to relieve her, but she sent him away and took Sundance for another walk. She didn't have the heart to go on with her day as though nothing were wrong. Before she knew it, two hours had passed. She pushed herself to her feet.

"Come on, Sundance, why don't you try to drink again?"

She led him to the waterer and stood there with him, talking to him and stroking his neck. Before long, he surprised her by dipping his lips in the water and taking a long drink. She nearly cried out in relief, but she checked herself, afraid of startling him and interrupting him.

"I see the patient is drinking. A very good sign!"

Leslie jumped and turned around in surprise. Dr. Burke was standing in the doorway with a medical bag in her hand.

Leslie smiled for the first time in hours.

"I'm so glad to see you! This is the first time I've been able to get him to drink."

"Has he passed anything yet?"

"Nothing."

The veterinarian examined Sundance, checking his gums, listening to his heart and stomach and performing various other procedures.

"Where's his owner?" she asked while she worked.

Leslie sighed, and her mouth turned down at the corners. "I don't know. I tried calling her, but she's mad at me, and her boyfriend wouldn't let her talk to me or even tell him what was wrong, so I called her mom, and I don't know if she'll ever get here."

"Well, that's all right. We'll take care of Mr. Sundance here, and I'll call her in a few minutes if she doesn't get here."

She was just straightening up after finishing her examination when Holly ran into the stall, asking, "Is he all right? What happened?"

"We don't really know yet, Holly, but Leslie and Helen have been taking excellent care of him. They gave him some things to help his digestion, and he had a drink a few minutes ago, so we just have to wait to see if he has a bowel movement. Once he does, he should be fine. It's just a waiting game now."

She paused to look at her watch.

"Since he's doing all right for now, I'm going to leave him to you while I go do another appointment. If he seems to get worse, or if he doesn't pass any manure in the next couple of hours, call me. Keep taking him for little walks until he seems to feel better, and you can give him some more mineral oil and probiotics."

She left the stall, and Leslie turned to her friend. They stared at each other for a moment, and then simultaneously threw their arms around each other and said, "I'm sorry! No, I'm sorry!" and then laughed.

Leslie released her hold and stepped back. "I never should have said anything. You were right; it was none of my business."

"No, you were right. Todd's a jerk, and you saw through him a long time ago. I should have known you wouldn't say anything like that unless you were really worried."

"Best friends again?"

"You bet!"

They hugged again, and Leslie smiled in relief and gratitude.

"So what happened? Todd wouldn't let me talk to you, but I knew you'd want to be here, so I called your mom and hoped she could get you the message."

A cloud passed over Holly's face. "Todd wouldn't let me answer the phone when you called, and then he took the phone when it rang again. I guess you must have called from the office or something. Anyway, we had this big fight about it, and I told him you were my best friend, and he couldn't talk to you that way."

Leslie's heart soared at the words.

Holly continued with, "We were at the batting cages,

and he told me to sit down and shut up until he was done hitting balls. I was so mad.

"Then Mom called and told me what was going on and I told Todd I had to get here, and he said that he was telling me for the last time that I was too old for horses and it was either him or Sundance, and if I didn't make the right choice he would never speak to me again."

Her eyes filled with tears, and Leslie felt truly sorry for her.

"So, I called my mom, but her car's in the shop and Daddy's at work. I had to take the bus here."

Leslie hugged her again. "I'm so sorry it turned out that way."

"Me too, but I'm extra sorry for how it affected you. And that it took Sundance getting sick for me to see through Todd."

"Speaking of Sundance, we should do what Dr. Burke said. We need to get him better!" Leslie said. She showed Holly how to use the turkey baster to squirt mineral oil into the back of his mouth and a smaller dosing syringe to give him probiotics.

"So, what exactly does this stuff do?" Holly asked.

"The mineral oil helps stuff to move through his gut and break up the blockage, and the probiotics help his digestion. Everything we're doing is supposed to help him move stuff through his intestines so he can poop and feel better. Now come on, it's your turn to take him for a walk."

The girls walked side by side, Holly leading Sundance. While they walked, Leslie told Holly all about what had happened with Alex and Kate at the dance. She had just finished the story when Sundance stopped, pulling on the lead line. They stopped and turned around.

"What's wrong, boy?" Holly asked.

In response, Sundance lifted his tail and pooped. The girls laughed and clapped and hugged each other.

"I've never been so happy to see poop in my entire life!" Holly said.

"Me neither," Leslie replied, a smile stretched across her face. "He's going to be just fine!"

"So are we," Holly added, and her smile was as genuine as Leslie's own.

Chapter Twelve:
The Schooling Show

The second Saturday in December was the Lost Lake Riders English schooling show. Helen was taking some of her younger students so they could participate, and Leslie decided to follow her stepmother's suggestion and show Spark. Holly couldn't attend because of a family function, but Alex said he would come along to help out and lend moral support.

Leslie briefly wondered if he was kissing up to make up for what had happened with Kate, then told herself she was being silly. Alex loved horse shows, and he enjoyed spending time with her.

"Do you think Kate will be there?" he asked the day before the show, while he and Leslie loaded the horse trailer with all of the tack and supplies the riders would need for the show. The weekend before, Leslie had taught the young riders how to clean their tack for the show; Helen liked her riders to be involved in the different aspects of owning and showing horses.

"I hope not. I just want to go have a good time with

Spark, and I want the kids to have fun. We don't need that spoiled brat coming around, making snide remarks and causing trouble."

Leslie felt the heat rise in her face when she thought about the pranks Kate had pulled on her earlier that year. Kate had tried everything to keep Leslie from succeeding in the show ring with Lucky, but in the end her efforts had failed.

"Leslie, take a deep breath. You're shaking!" Leslie came out of her reverie. Alex's hands were on her arms and his eyes were round with alarm.

"Sorry, I just got caught up thinking about all the lousy stuff she's done to me this year." She shook herself, willing away the unpleasant thoughts. "Anyway, I'm going to try not to think about her. Let's put our energy into making sure everything is ready."

"So, are you excited to be showing Spark tomorrow?" Alex asked, changing the subject.

"*So* excited. He's been doing really well, and he's such a sweet horse. I really like him. It's just..." her voice trailed off and she bit her lip, looking down at the box she was holding.

"Just what? Are you afraid you'll fall off or something?"

Leslie smiled and glanced up at him, then back at the box.

"No, no. Nothing like that. It's just that—" she took a deep breath and continued. "I'm afraid someone will recognize him, and I'll have to give him back to his real owner. As much as I like him, I can't ever forget the fact that he's not really my horse."

Alex took the box out of her hands and set it down so he could wrap his arms around her, and she laid her head on his shoulder gratefully. "It'll be OK, Leslie. I know you like him, and I do, too. Hopefully, you'll get to keep him."

Leslie squeezed back and answered in a small voice, "Thanks, Alex. I hope so too."

She stood there in his arms for another moment or two, then cleared her throat and broke the hug.

"I guess we should get back to work. The trailer isn't going to load itself!"

Leslie and Alex worked together to make sure everything was in the horse trailer, checking off the needed items from a list to make sure they didn't forget anything. When that task was finished, Leslie taught Alex how to use the clippers to make the horses look neat and trim. She started with Copper, a pony one of the kids would be riding.

"Since this is a schooling show, we won't give them a full-on clip job like we would for a rated show," Leslie said. "Since rated shows—the official shows that qualify you for regionals and nationals—have stiffer competition, you want your horse to look the best they possibly can. At a schooling show, looks are not as important. A lot of the horses are not registered or even purebred of any breed. Most of the people showing here are just getting some experience or having fun."

"So why are we doing this at all?"

Leslie rolled her eyes. "It is a horse show, silly! Making sure our horses are clean and well presented is part of it—and part of the fun! It's like dressing up to go out on a date. You didn't go on our first date in dirty old jeans and unbrushed hair!"

Alex laughed. "Well, that's true. I guess I see your point."

"Let's start with the bridle path. I usually use a forty

blade for this. The bigger the number on the blade, the closer it cuts. A forty gives a nice, close cut."

She used the clippers to neatly shave the pony's mane just behind his ears.

"How do you know how long to make it?"

"In open competitions, like at this schooling show, the bridle path is usually the length of the horse's ear," Leslie answered. "With Arabians, we tend to like them a little longer than that. Copper here is half Arabian and half Welsh, so I keep his bridle path a little longer than his ear."

Next, she clipped Copper's long whiskers around his muzzle and eyes, and then switched to a ten blade to remove the little brushes of hair on his fetlocks, the joint just above the hooves.

"We don't want him to look like a goat!" she quipped.

"He looks much better," Alex said, looking at the pony appraisingly. "Can I do the next one?"

"Definitely, and I'll watch to make sure you don't make any mistakes. When spring and show season get closer, I'll show you how to do a fancier show clip, but this is good practice to start with. You have to be really careful, because if you clip in the wrong place or use the wrong blade, you can give them unsightly bald patches or cut off hair you're not supposed to — hair that takes a long time to grow back."

Leslie watched while Alex clipped the other three horses going to the show, including Spark. It was not a difficult job, and with Leslie's guidance he managed to finish it without making any mistakes. When he was done, it was time for dinner, and Alex's mother had arrived to take him home.

The next morning, Leslie awoke at dawn and ate a

bowl of cereal before walking out to the barn. She and Helen had decided not to bathe the horses for the show, because between the cold weather and their long coats, it would take them too long to dry and they could become sick. Instead, the riders would groom the horses thoroughly at the show.

Since she and Alex had loaded the trailer the night before, there was not much left to do except put the horses' shipping bandages on, put them in the trailer, and go to the show. Although she had plenty of time to do that, Leslie felt restless. She felt the need to check the trailer again to make sure it was securely hitched and everything was loaded, and when she was satisfied, she gathered the shipping wraps and put them on the horses to protect their legs during the short trip to the show.

When everything was done, it was still half an hour before Helen had planned to leave for the show and Alex had not arrived yet. Leslie decided to walk out to the pasture to visit Lucky.

Juan and Josh had already fed, so Lucky was eating. Leslie's heart lifted when he nickered at her and left his breakfast to greet her at the gate. She let herself inside and wrapped her arms around his neck.

"Lucky, I hope you don't mind I'm showing another horse today."

She scratched his withers and he stretched his upper lip out in appreciation. She giggled and patted him on the shoulder.

"OK, boy, go back to your breakfast. Wish Spark and me luck!"

By the time she arrived back at the barn, Helen and Alex were there, waiting for her.

"It looks like you have everything all ready to go,"

Helen said happily. "Great job! Let's get the horses loaded, and then we can go. The students are meeting us at the show with their families, so I don't want to be late."

Leslie and Alex loaded the horses into the trailer one at a time while Helen made sure she had all of her paperwork in order, and then they climbed into the cab of the truck to make the short journey to the show grounds. It was not a long distance and traffic was light, so they arrived at their destination in about fifteen minutes.

While she drove, Helen asked, "So, Leslie, have you decided how many classes you want to enter?"

"I think I'll just do two," Leslie responded, looking over the show's class list in her hand. "I don't want to overwhelm Spark at his first show, assuming it is actually his first show."

"That sounds like a good plan," her stepmother agreed.

"Are you going to do equitation or pleasure?" Alex asked.

"Just pleasure classes, since they're judged on the horse. It wouldn't be very fair for me to show in equitation at a schooling show, since I was National Champion earlier this year!"

Equitation classes, Leslie's favorite, are judged on the rider's performance, while pleasure classes are judged on the horse.

"I think that's very sportsmanlike of you, Leslie," Helen said approvingly. "Some riders would go ahead and enter, knowing they can win. It's nice of you to give other kids a chance."

Leslie blushed at the compliment. "Thanks, Mom. It just seemed like the right thing to do."

"That's one of the things I admire about both of you,

Alex and Leslie," Helen said. "When it comes to doing kind things for others, you do it without even thinking about it."

Leslie blushed and looked at Alex out of the corner of her eye and saw that his cheeks had turned pink too. He cleared his throat and changed the subject, clearly uncomfortable with the fuss Helen made. "So, uh, what are you going to do if someone recognizes Spark?"

Leslie frowned, feeling the heat drain out of her cheeks. "Well, then I guess we'll do what we need to do to verify he belongs to whoever claims him, and then I guess we'll give him back. As much as I've grown attached to him, I can't keep a horse who doesn't belong to me."

"I just hope if they take him back, they take better care of him," Alex said.

"If his real owner does decide they want him back, I will check into them thoroughly," Helen put in kindly. "I'll make sure they take care of Spark, and check up on him from time to time to make sure he's OK. Would that set your minds at ease?"

"Really? You would do that?" Leslie asked, feeling optimistic.

"Sure. I kind of like Spark myself, and I wouldn't want to see him go back to a bad home. I think he's already been through enough. But let's not worry about it until the time comes. We don't even know that anyone will recognize him."

Helen turned down the driveway that led to the show grounds, and the conversation was over. Alex and Leslie jumped out of the truck as soon as it came to a stop and immediately set to the task of pulling the horses out of the trailer, tying them up and removing their shipping bandages. The day was uncharacteristically warm for December, chilly enough for a jacket but not freezing.

The students arrived a few minutes later, and Leslie went with them to the horse show office to help them sign up for their classes. The mothers trailed along behind, chatting excitedly. This was the first horse show for the three little girls and their families. The girls skipped along in their high boots, breeches and hunt coats. Leslie smiled at how they giggled and chattered about the ribbons they hoped to win.

"I want to win a red one!"

"Why? Blue is better."

"But red is my favorite color."

"Red is second place. Don't you want to win first place?"

"What color is first place?"

"Blue."

"Oooh, I want a blue ribbon!"

Leslie giggled. At the office, she showed the girls how to fill out their forms with their names, horses' names and the classes they wanted to enter, then filled out her own and paid her money. When everyone had finished, they walked back to the trailers to get their horses ready.

Alex, Helen and Leslie helped the girls groom the horses until every speck of dirt was removed and then tack them up. They finished with fifteen minutes to spare before the show started, which was just enough time to warm up their horses.

Once the riders made sure their helmets were on and numbers were pinned to the backs of their jackets, they mounted and rode to the warm-up arena.

"How come your outfit is different than ours, Leslie?" one of the girls asked while they walked to the warm-up arena. Leslie looked down at her long coat that reached her knees and matching pants that extended past her boot heels.

"I'm riding saddle seat, and you're riding hunt seat. See how my bridle has two bits, while yours only has one, and my saddle is flatter than yours? Spark likes to pick his knees and hocks up high, like Lucky, so he gets to be a saddle seat horse."

"I want to ride saddle seat like you!" the girl frowned, although the corners of her mouth didn't stay down for very long. The excitement of the show still sparkled in her eyes.

"And some day you will! Right now, though, your horse is a great hunt seat horse. You should enjoy him."

The girl nodded slowly. "I guess you're right. Do you get to show in the same classes we do, or do they have special classes for saddle seat?"

"At this show, they have all the English riders together, whether they ride hunt seat or saddle seat. At Arabian horse shows, they have separate classes for the different styles."

They arrived at the warm-up arena and each turned to concentrate on her own horse. Helen stationed herself in the center and called out orders while her students rode around the edge of the arena. They walked, trotted and cantered in each direction to practice and make sure their horses were loosened up and ready to do their best in the show.

When she thought Spark was ready, Leslie asked him to walk and let him stretch out his neck and relax. She let her eyes wander, looking at the various horses and riders around her. There were a few faces she recognized, although no one she knew personally. She was happy to see that Kate was not there, at least not that she could see. She did notice a young man with red hair and freckles standing by the fence who was watching her a lot, but she tried not to stare at him.

Maybe he just thinks Spark is pretty. Maybe he doesn't recognize him, she thought, trying to reassure herself. She stroked Spark's neck nervously.

She rode into the center of the arena and halted by Helen.

"He looks good," her stepmother said. "I think he's going to be a good boy for you."

"I think so too. I just want this to be a good experience today."

Leslie fiddled with her reins for a moment, and then slyly looked at the fence where her watcher was standing to see if he was still there. He was, and he was still staring at her.

"Um, Mom? Don't look now, but there's a red-haired man leaning against the fence over there, who's been staring at me. I'm wondering if he recognizes Spark."

Helen watched a student go by, letting her gaze rest momentarily on the man by the fence before turning to make sure Leslie's girth was tight enough.

"You're right, he is staring at you. Well, don't panic yet. Maybe he just really likes how you ride. You're pretty good you know," she said. She winked and patted Leslie's leg.

"Only because I had a good teacher." Leslie winked back.

"Five minute call for class number one, English Pleasure Novice," a voice boomed over the speaker system. "If you're in class number one, please make your way to the in-gate now."

"You're in that class, right?" Helen asked, and Leslie

nodded in reply. "OK, go on and head over to the gate. I need to round up the kids and get them over, too."

Leslie gathered up her reins and rode toward the in-gate, trying not to think about the man who was watching her. However, she could not stop herself from thinking about him and wondering if he was Spark's real owner, or knew his real owner.

This could be my last time riding Spark, she thought, frowning.

"Leslie, what are you doing? The gate is open. You need to go in your class!" Helen's voice snapped Leslie out of her thoughts.

She looked around and saw all the other riders had already gone into the arena, so she hurriedly gathered her reins and pushed Spark into a trot. He obliged, and they swept through the gate and into the arena.

Leslie was only half paying attention when she trotted into the arena on Spark. She did not know how many other horses were in the class or where they were, only that her horse was beneath her. After she had made one complete circuit of the arena, she saw the red-haired man standing by the gate and watching her. Leslie was distracted, so wrapped up in her concerns and watching the man out of the corner of her eye that she was not doing her best. She did not keep Spark's head and neck properly arched in a head set, neither did she keep him moving out as smartly as he could.

Because she was not looking where she was going, she allowed herself to get in the middle of a pack of other riders, where the judge could not see her. Thanks to her distraction, when it was time for the awards, her name and Spark's were called for fifth place—ahead of just three other riders.

Leslie sighed and patted the horse on the neck.

"I'm sorry, boy. That was my fault. You were a gem, like you always are. Next class, I'll pay more attention. I promise."

She collected her ribbon and rode out of the arena. Helen's other three students had placed first, second and third in the class, so they had already gathered at the trainer by the time Leslie reached her. Alex stood nearby, looking bemused.

"Leslie! Leslie! I got a red ribbon, just like I wanted!"

Leslie laughed. It seemed the girl had already forgotten she had changed her wish to a blue ribbon.

"Congratulations, girls! I'm so proud of you!"

Alex reached out his hands to take the ribbons from each of them. "Great job, girls! I'll go hang these on the trailer for you." Once he had collected all four, he walked over to the horse trailer with them.

"Ooh Leslie, you got a pink ribbon. It's so pretty!" said the girl who had won the class.

"Thank you. I really like the blue ones the best, but I'm glad you got it this time, Cindy."

"OK, girls, it's time for your class for riders thirteen and under. Leslie and I will watch you, OK?"

The little girls nodded and trotted off toward the in-gate, which had just opened to start their class. Helen turned to Leslie, her face creased with concern.

"What happened in there, Leslie? You weren't paying attention, you weren't riding your horse, and you allowed yourself to get buried. You know the judge can't place you if he can't see you. That wasn't like you."

"I'm sorry, Mom. It's just that I can't get that man out of my head, and he was watching me the whole time. I was really distracted."

Helen nodded. "I thought that might be the problem, because I know you know better. Just try to put him out of your mind and concentrate better in your next class, OK?"

Leslie took a deep breath, let it out and nodded.

"All right, then. Let's go watch the girls in their class."

Leslie rode and Helen walked toward the fence where they could watch the class in the arena. Helen called out encouragement and instructions to her students as they rode by, and they all did very well, capturing the top three places once again. This time, however, the places were switched around so each girl received different ribbons than the class before.

Leslie managed to forget the red-haired man, because she was so wrapped up in watching her fellow students. Alex returned from the trailer and stood next to Leslie while they watched, his arm resting on her leg.

When all of the ribbons for their class had been handed out, it was time for Leslie's next class. She gathered her reins, resolved to pay attention to her horse and what she was doing, and rode toward the in-gate.

"Good luck!" Helen and Alex called to her.

Leslie called "Thank you!" over her shoulder, and then she rode through the gate.

Leslie looked around her to see where the other horses were so she could keep herself and Spark out of trouble and in the judge's view. She squeezed Spark with her legs and the reins with her fingers, and he arched his neck and strode out in a nice trot. Leslie was so caught up in riding Spark to the best of her ability and watching for traffic that she forgot all about the red-haired man. She did not even look for him on the rail as she moved around the arena.

Spark did everything she asked of him and did not make any mistakes. Leslie was thrilled when she pulled into the lineup with the other riders at the end of the class.

"Good boy!" she exclaimed, patting Spark on the neck. "We should place a little better this time, which should make up for my embarrassing you in the first class."

Her suspicion came true, and she was awarded a first place ribbon. Leslie's heart soared, and she had a large grin on her face.

"I knew we could do it, boy!"

She gave him a big hug around his neck before she rode forward to collect her ribbon and the jar of horse cookies that were the prize for first place.

Helen and Alex were waiting for her just outside of the gate, and Leslie jumped off Spark and threw her arms around his neck again, then Alex's, then Helen's. "We did it! He was such a good boy!"

"Good job, Leslie!" Helen's face was all smiles, and her eyes sparkled with pride. "You rode that class like I know you're capable of, and look how it came out!"

"I know. You were right. I just needed to forget about everything else and concentrate on what I was doing."

"I'm proud of you, Leslie," Alex said, kissing her on the cheek. "You've done a really good job with Spark."

No sooner than the words were out of his mouth when the red-haired man approached them. A lump rose in Leslie's throat, and the sparkle left her eyes.

I guess I'll find out what this is all about now, she thought.

"Excuse me," he said politely.

"Hello," Helen said. Leslie and Alex stared at him, waiting in silence.

"I hope you don't mind my intrusion," he said, reaching his hand out to allow Spark to sniff it. "But I just had to ask you about this horse. Is this Sirius, Nancy Miller's horse?"

Helen, Alex and Leslie looked at each other, and Leslie looked down at her boots. When she could not find the words to answer, Helen spoke up.

"Actually, Leslie found this horse in the forest near my farm during the fire. He had obviously been abandoned for some time, because he was very thin and his feet were in very bad shape. Leslie has been working very hard to rehabilitate him.

"We've advertised that we found him, but no one has claimed him so I gave Leslie permission to show him. Do you recognize him?"

"He looks very much like Nancy's horse. If it is him, she owned his mother and raised him from a baby. She had him professionally trained and was going to show him, but then she was diagnosed with cancer. She's very elderly, and I thought she might have sold him to you. He was her last horse, and she loved him like he was her own child."

Leslie felt her chest tighten.

If this Nancy Miller is his owner, she doesn't sound like someone who would abandon a horse, she thought.

She found the words to speak and said, "Do you know how to contact Mrs. Miller? We should let her know Spark, I mean Sirius, is safe. Maybe he ran away from home, and she couldn't find him."

"I can give you her address and phone number, if you have something to write with," he answered.

"If you follow us back to our trailer, I have some paper and a pen," Helen said. While they walked, she asked, "May I ask how you know Mrs. Miller?"

"She's a good friend of my family, although I haven't seen her in a few months. The poor lady doesn't have any family left, so she spends a lot of time alone."

"That's so sad," Leslie said. She imagined the sick old woman living by herself and hoped she would never be in that position herself.

"Here, Leslie," Alex put in softly. "I'll take care of Spark so you can get Mrs. Miller's information."

"Thanks, Alex," Leslie answered, handing him the reins.

She went to the passenger door of the truck and retrieved a small notepad and pen from the glove compartment.

"Here you go, um..." she trailed off, realizing the red-haired man had not introduced himself.

"Sean," he said, smiling. He wrote down the information and handed the pad and pen back to Leslie. "Best of luck. You've done a great job with him."

"Thanks," Leslie said, and waved goodbye while he walked away. When she stopped waving, her resolve crumbled and she burst into tears. Helen was immediately there, enveloping Leslie in a hug.

"Shh it's OK, Leslie. We'll go talk to Mrs. Miller and see if she'd be willing to sell him to us. I don't want to give him back any more than you do," she said soothingly.

"But—but, he said Spark was her last horse, and she's had him since he was a baby and she loves him. Why would she sell him?" There was a hitch in Leslie's voice, and she tried to get herself under control.

"He also said she's very old and sick. She may not be able to take care of Spark anymore. After all, he did end up in the woods, didn't he?"

Leslie sniffed and nodded. "OK, maybe you're right. I guess I should try to be positive."

"That's my girl. Now you sit here and try to pull yourself together, then you can come help us. But first, you need to fold up your pant legs."

She pointed at Leslie's feet, and Leslie groaned. She had forgotten to roll up the legs of her long pants when she dismounted, and they had gotten dirty when she walked around with them dragging. She brushed them off as well as she could and rolled them up, chastising herself for her carelessness. Leslie leaned against the truck and took a few deep breaths, then wiped away her tears and went to help the others. All of the riders were done for the day, so all they had to do was pack up, load the horses and head home.

The little girls were ready to leave with their mothers. They all swarmed around Helen, hugging her and thanking her for the lessons and helping them win ribbons, and then they converged on Leslie.

"Thanks for helping us, Leslie!"

"I hope you feel better soon, Leslie!"

"Congratulations on your pretty ribbons, Leslie!"

She hugged them all back by turn, enjoying their sunny personalities. "Thank *you*, girls. You did a great job today!"

They waved goodbye, climbed into their cars and were gone. Leslie turned to Helen and said, "Those three little girls are just the sweetest, funnest little girls I've ever known!"

"They sure are," Helen answered. "I feel very fortunate to have them as students."

She stopped and looked thoughtful for a moment before adding, "In fact, I only have good students... now. Everyone is willing to pitch in when they need to, and they all have good attitudes. None of them are spoiled, and I really appreciate that."

Leslie couldn't help but smirk, knowing Helen probably was referring to Kate, but she was too kind to say so.

With the three of them working together, they were ready to go in minutes. Helen made one last check of all the doors on the trailer to make sure they were closed securely, and they were on their way home.

Leslie's spirits had lifted with the distractions of the little girls and packing up, but when silence fell in the cab of the truck, her thoughts turned back to Spark and Nancy Miller.

"Do you think we could call Mrs. Miller tonight, Mom?" she asked.

Helen looked at her briefly with eyebrows raised in surprise. "Are you sure? I wouldn't think you'd be very anxious for him to go back to his owner."

Leslie shrugged. "I'm not, but I can't stand not knowing anymore. I need to know for sure whether he's leaving so I can come to terms with it. Besides, I'm still holding out hope she'll let me keep him. Like you said, she is old and sick, so maybe she can't take care of him anymore, and that's why he ran away."

Helen reached over and squeezed Leslie's hand.

"That's my girl. Think positive."

Alex squeezed Leslie's other hand, and they drove home that way, in silence, each lost in their own thoughts.

Chapter Thirteen:
Nancy Miller

The evening after the schooling show, when everything was put away and all the chores were done, Leslie sat in front of the telephone in the living room, staring at the piece of paper with Nancy Miller's information on it in her hand.

"You've been sitting there for half an hour, Leslie," her father's voice sounded from over her shoulder. "Are you going to call her?"

His voice was gentle and reassuring.

Leslie sighed and kept her eyes glued to the phone. "Yes. I want to get this over with, but at the same time, I dread it. Does that make sense?"

Dan sat next to Leslie on the couch and put his arm around her shoulders. "It makes perfect sense. You want the closure, but you're afraid you won't get the closure you want. But, honey, you know this is something you have to do. Spark belongs to Mrs. Miller, and she deserves to know you have him."

"I know, Dad." Leslie sighed.

"Will it help if I sit here with you while you do it?"

Leslie looked at him, at his deep brown eyes filled with concern, and nodded.

"Yeah, that would help. Thank you."

She took a deep breath and dialed the phone.

The line rang, and Leslie's heart pounded. It rang four times, and then the answering machine picked up.

"You've reached the Miller residence," a friendly but shaky female voice said. "We're probably out feeding the horses, so please leave a message and we'll call you back as soon as we can."

There was a long beep, and then silence.

Leslie had not been expecting an answering machine. She froze, not sure what to say, while the machine waited. Finally, she blurted out, "Um, hello. My name is Leslie Clark and I think I may have found your horse, Sirius." Leslie left her phone number and then finished with, "Um, thanks."

She hung up quickly and stared at the phone again, as though she expected it to suddenly come to life.

Dan squeezed her shoulders. "There, was that so bad? She'll probably call you back in a day or two, and then we can get this settled. "

Leslie heaved a heavy sigh. "I guess not. I guess I can keep hoping until she calls me back."

However, Nancy Miller did not call back in a day or two. Leslie jumped every time the phone rang, her stomach in knots, but it was never the call she was waiting for. Once it was Holly on the other end of the line, and Leslie could not hide her disappointment.

"Oh, hey, Holly."

Holly laughed. "Well, don't sound so excited to hear from me!"

"I'm sorry, Holly. I've just been waiting on pins and needles ever since I learned who Spark's real owner is."

She had already explained to Holly how Sean had approached her at the show and gave her Nancy Miller's contact information.

"I can understand why you're so upset. I'd be pretty anxious too. Anyway, I was calling to see if you wanted to go for a trail ride this afternoon? It hasn't rained in a few days, so the trails should be good."

Leslie hesitated. "I don't know, Holly. I should probably stay by the phone in case Mrs. Miller calls."

"You have an answering machine, don't you? "

"Well, yeah...but—"

"But nothing. You ever hear that phrase, 'a watched pot never boils'? The same thing goes for telephones. They never ring while you're watching them."

Leslie could not help but laugh at her friend's logic. "But I was watching it when you called!"

Holly hesitated for only a beat before answering, "That doesn't count. I wasn't the call you were waiting for, remember? Come on, getting out for a bit will distract you so you don't drive yourself crazy. Besides, I'm dying to go for a ride!"

"I have to admit you have a point. Can you come over now?"

"Sure. Give me twenty minutes."

Leslie had Spark saddled and ready to go by the time Holly arrived, and she helped her friend get Sundance ready. Soon they were on the trail, the horses bobbing their heads merrily. While they rode, Leslie told Holly more about the schooling show. When she started talking about Sean and Mrs. Miller again, Holly changed the subject.

"So have you done any of your Christmas shopping yet? It's only a couple weeks away."

"No, I haven't even started. I haven't had time! I don't even know what to get anyone."

They discussed gift possibilities for Dan, Helen and Alex, as well as what Holly was getting for her family, for the rest of the trail ride. When they returned to the barn and Leslie heard the phone in the office ring, she abruptly realized she had not thought of Mrs. Miller for the entire two hours she and Holly had been riding. She stopped in the barn aisle and waited anxiously while Julie answered the call, and she dropped back into her funk when she learned it was not Mrs. Miller.

"This could be the last time I ride you, boy," she said sadly, patting Spark on the neck. Holly looked at her with sympathy, and the two girls untacked their horses and put them away in silence.

"Thanks for the ride, Leslie," Holly said as she gave Leslie a hug. "Good luck with that lady. Let me know when you finally talk to her, OK?"

"Will do," Leslie said, hugging her friend tight. They released their hold and Holly ran out to the parking lot, where her mother waited in the car.

On the evening of the third day after she had left the message on Nancy Miller's machine, Leslie was a nervous wreck. She could barely think of anything else, and her chores and homework suffered for the lack of attention. She was distracted in school, and her teachers seemed determined to humiliate her by calling on her when she was not paying attention—much to the amusement of her classmates, especially Kate.

That night at dinner, Leslie was lost in thought when her father tapped her on the arm.

"Huh? What?" she asked, looking around and suddenly realizing her father and Helen were staring at her.

"Leslie, you've been holding that forkful of mashed potatoes for about five minutes, and your father has asked for the butter three times," Helen said gently.

"Oh, sorry," Leslie mumbled. She put the mashed potatoes in her mouth, and then laid her fork down so she could hand the butter to her father.

Her parents looked at each other. Dan said, "Leslie, maybe you should go ahead and call her again. Maybe you could try calling a couple more times without leaving a message, to see if she picks up."

Leslie shrugged. "OK, maybe that is a good idea. I'll call after dinner."

Leslie went into the living room after dinner and dialed Mrs. Miller's phone number, but there was still no answer.

She called every evening after that, but there was still no answer. On Saturday afternoon, a week after Leslie had left her message on Mrs. Miller's machine, Dan offered to drive her over to Mrs. Miller's house to see if they could catch her at home.

"I think that would be a good idea," Leslie answered, nodding. "As long as Mom doesn't need me?"

She looked hopefully at Helen, who nodded. "You go ahead, Leslie. I'll finish up here and you can fill me in later, OK?"

"OK." Leslie wrapped her arms around her stepmother. "Wish me luck?"

Helen squeezed her tight before answering, "Good luck, Leslie. Stay positive."

"Thanks, Mom."

Leslie climbed into the car with her father, and they

headed toward the address Sean had written for Mrs. Miller's house.

"I got a map off the Internet," Dan said, "and it shouldn't take more than about fifteen minutes to get there."

Leslie stared out the window during the trip, barely noticing the trees and houses that whizzed by. She was too busy trying to imagine what Nancy Miller was like and wondering whether the woman would be willing to let Leslie keep Spark. They were the same thoughts and what-ifs that had been plaguing her ever since Spark had found his temporary home at Green Meadow. It seemed like years had passed since the fire, instead of just three months.

When Dan pulled down the dirt driveway, Leslie focused her eyes on the scene outside the window.

"Are you sure this is the right place?" she asked in astonishment.

The place was run down, with broken fences, a barn that looked like it should be condemned and a house that didn't look much better. There were no animals in evidence, and the car looked like it hadn't moved in years, with four flat tires and a layer of dust so thick she couldn't tell what color it was supposed to be.

Dan looked at his map and answered, "This is the address Sean gave you, and there was a sign on the gatepost that said Miller. I hate to tell you this, but I think this is the place."

Leslie looked at her father, and he looked back with concern in his eyes. "If it is, I don't see how she could take care of Spark. This place doesn't look fit to keep a chicken, let alone a horse. Or people, for that matter."

"I don't know much about keeping animals, as you

know, but I have to agree with you. It looks like Mrs. Miller needs some help," he answered.

"I think you're right. Maybe we should talk to her about getting some while we're here. Sean said she doesn't have any family left, poor lady."

"OK, let's go knock on the door and take it from there," Dan said, opening his door and climbing out. Leslie followed him, and they walked together up the creaking steps to the front door of the house. Dan knocked, and they waited, staring at the peeling paint on the door.

I think it was blue once, but it's hard to tell, Leslie thought. She let her eyes wander over the cracked, dust-covered windows and the broken glider on the porch. When there was no answer after a couple of minutes, Dan knocked again, louder than before. He tried several more times, and still there was no answer.

Father and daughter looked at each other questioningly.

"What should we do? Come back another day?" Leslie asked.

"I don't know, Les. I have a bad feeling about this. Mrs. Miller is very old and sick. If she is in there, she probably needs help." He tried the doorknob, and it turned stiffly in his hand. "The door is unlocked. I'm going to go in and see what I can find out. Why don't you stay out here?"

His face was a mask of grim determination. Leslie noticed an odd, unpleasant odor coming from inside.

Leslie looked around again. "OK. I'll just sit on the steps and keep an eye out for anyone coming up the drive."

She sat on the creaking steps and waited while he

went inside. She could hear him calling, "Mrs. Miller?" softly inside the house.

She glanced around the yard and took in the tire swing hanging from a tree with the tire that sagged badly with age and the swing set that was covered in rust and half buried in weeds.

There were once children here, she thought sadly. *I wonder how long ago?*

The road from which Mrs. Miller's driveway stemmed was not a busy one. Only one car drove by while Leslie sat there, and it did not turn down the driveway. It was a few minutes before her father stepped quietly back out onto the porch and closed the door behind him.

"Leslie," he said somberly, sitting down next to her. "I have something to tell you."

Leslie looked at him, and his eyes were filled with tears.

Her stomach turned over. "What is it, Dad?"

Dan looked at his hands, clenched between his knees. "Leslie, there's no easy way to say this. Mrs. Miller is... gone."

Leslie furrowed her brow and studied his profile. "What do you mean? She's not here? I don't understand — what's the matter?"

"Leslie," he started again, looking around the yard, then at her, "what I mean is, Mrs. Miller passed away."

"What? How do you know?" She looked over her shoulder at the closed door, then back at him.

He was looking at his hands again. "Leslie, she's still in there. In fact, it looks like she's been in there, uh, passed away, for a long time."

Leslie's stomach churned at the thought of what lay

inside the house behind her.

"Oh, God," she murmured, fingertips flying to her mouth.

Her father heaved a heavy sigh. "I'm sorry to have to tell you this, Leslie. It's very unfortunate and, well, grisly."

Leslie nodded.

"Well. I guess that explains some things." The corners of her mouth turned down and her eyes filled. "Oh, Dad!" she leaned into his chest and he wrapped his arms around her while she cried. "That poor woman!"

She couldn't keep the thoughts and pictures of Mrs. Miller dying alone from running through her head.

"Shh, it's OK, Les. Don't cry." He rocked her back and forth and stroked her hair.

"But, Dad," she choked out, "it's just so sad! She's been living all alone for who knows how long, and then she died, and no one even knew!"

"I know. It's hard to be left all alone in the world."

"And all this time, we've been talking about how cruel his real owner was for abandoning him. She didn't abandon him at all! She loved him, and she died, and he was left all alone. Can you imagine how he must have felt, standing in his paddock, day after day, with no food or water, waiting for her to come take care of him? It's so awful!"

Tears finally overcame her and she was no longer able to continue.

Dan held her for a while until she had cried herself out, and then a little longer, until she decided she had the strength to take care of the situation they faced.

She drew in a deep, shuddering breath and let it out, wiped her eyes and pulled out of his embrace.

"Should we do something for poor old Mrs. Miller? Is there someone we should call?"

Dan nodded, pulling out his cell phone. "I'll call the police department and let them take care of it. We'd better not leave yet, though, just in case they have any questions for us. I'm sorry to make you stay here even a minute longer, but I'm afraid it's necessary."

Leslie didn't want to stay in that abysmal place any longer than she had to, but she knew he was probably right. "That's OK, Dad. I know it's what we have to do. I just hope the police hurry."

Dan made the call, explaining to the person at the other end of the line what he had found and why they were there in the first place. He hung up a few minutes later and told Leslie, "They're sending someone over as soon as they can, but it might be a bit of a wait. They did ask us to stay here so they can take statements from us."

Leslie shuddered. "Let's just get away from the house, OK?" She didn't want to think about what lay inside. "Do you think we could take a look around while we wait?"

"Sure, just let me call Helen first to tell her what's going on."

He made the call and explained to Helen what he had found and that the police were on their way, then they joined hands and walked toward the barn. They stopped at the entrance and peered inside the dark, musty interior.

"We need to be really careful," Dan said. "This place doesn't look very stable."

Leslie nearly smiled at his unintentional pun but was too sad. Instead she nodded, looking at the cracked and rotted boards that made up the walls. Inside, she could see cobwebs in every corner. There were indistinct shapes on the floor, covered in tarps laden with dirt. Broken boards and beams littered the floor or hung from the ceiling.

"I don't think I want to go in there," Leslie said, leading her father toward the paddocks. "I don't think any animals have lived in there in a long time."

"I think you might be right," Dan said.

All of the paddocks outside were in bad disrepair, with gates off their hinges, fences falling down and water troughs overturned. The one closest to the house was in the best shape, with the only damage a dislodged top rail from one of the fences.

Looking it over, Leslie said, "This must have been Spark's home. It looks like the only one that was even close to being suitable for keeping a horse. He must have pushed down the rail of the fence there and jumped out when she stopped taking care of him." Leslie felt a lump rising in her throat and fought to swallow it back. "Poor Spark. I wonder how long he waited for her."

A few minutes later, a patrol car pulled into the driveway and parked in front of the house. Dan and Leslie walked over to meet the officer who climbed out.

"I'm Dan Clark, and this is my daughter, Leslie," he said, shaking the officer's hand. His voice was somber, with none of his usual humor.

"Nice to meet you, although I wish it was under better circumstances," the officer said solemnly. He shook both of their hands. "I just need to ask you a few questions, and then I'll check out the house. What relationship are you to the deceased?"

Leslie started to speak, but a lump rose in her throat and she knew she couldn't get the words out. She turned pleading eyes to her father for help. He explained why they were at the house, and the officer took notes, stopping Dan from time to time to clarify what happened. He took down their names, address and phone number, and then went inside the house to see Mrs. Miller's remains and assess the situation.

When he stepped back out onto the porch, he said, "I think I have all I need from you two, so you're free to go. We may be in touch if anything comes up, and someone may contact you about her horse if anyone has a legitimate claim to him."

"Officer," Dan began, "my daughter has been taking care of this horse for the past three months. She saved him from a fire and has done a wonderful job rehabilitating him—he was quite emaciated when she found him. Is there any way she can keep him?"

The officer looked kindly at Leslie and answered, "You certainly make a good case if there are no heirs. However, I think it's only fair to be honest with you. If someone has a lien on him for some reason, maybe for unpaid veterinary bills or the like, they may go so far as to take you to court to take him so they can sell him to cover the unpaid bill."

Leslie nodded her understanding, although she was not happy to hear his news. "I understand. I guess I'll just keep hoping for the best."

The officer's eyes softened. He put his hand on her shoulder and he said kindly, "Try not to worry. If there's anything I can do to help you keep your horse, I'll do it. You did a good thing, and you should be rewarded for it."

Leslie smiled, her heart lifting a little. "Thank you, officer. I've really become attached to him, even though I knew he belonged to someone else all along."

The officer smiled. "I understand. My daughter has a horse, and I've never seen a stronger bond between two creatures than I do between them. So, I know what it's like to love a horse. Keep your chin up, OK?"

He chucked her softly on the chin and winked.

"Will do, officer. Thank you for everything." Dan reached out to shake the officer's hand. "Call us when you have any updates. Thank you for coming out so quickly."

They said their goodbyes, and then Dan and Leslie climbed into the car to go home.

Chapter Fourteen:
Christmas

If Leslie thought waiting for Mrs. Miller to return her call was hard, waiting to see if someone would lay claim to Spark was even harder. She continued to ride him, hoping her efforts would be rewarded and he would stay with her forever.

"But what if someone comes and takes him away? All your effort will be for nothing," Alex said one day while he helped her untack and groom Spark after a training session.

"It won't be for nothing at all," Leslie said, gazing affectionately at the horse's finely sculpted face and planting a kiss on his nose. He sniffed her face and bumped her lightly with his muzzle. "I love spending time with him, and he deserves to look and feel the best he possibly can in case someone does claim him. If they want to sell him, he'll go to a better home if he looks like a show horse and his training is up to date."

"I can see your point. How long do you think it'll be

before you know anything?"

"Hard to say. The state will try to find Mrs. Miller's heirs, and if they do, they'll turn everything over to them. Spark would legally belong to them. If they don't find any heirs, the court will decide what to do with her property, including Spark. If anyone has a lien against her for some reason, like an unpaid vet or farrier bill, they could potentially claim Spark to cover her bill. If no one claims him, the court could turn him over to Animal Control, but Dad says that since I've been taking care of him so long, they'd probably just let me keep him, and then I would have to convince the registry to turn over his papers to me."

She sighed and added, "It could be months before the whole thing is settled."

"That stinks," Alex said with a frown. "There are so many ways this can go; there's just no saying."

"I couldn't agree more."

When Christmas was only a week away, Leslie realized she had been so busy with school and horses that she had not had time to go Christmas shopping. Christmas vacation had started, so she had a little bit of time for herself. She brought up the subject at breakfast.

"If you want to invite Alex or Holly to go with you, I'll drop you off at the mall and pick you up," Dan said. It was Sunday and he was off work.

"That would be great!" She turned to her stepmother and added, "That is, if you don't need me, Mom?"

Helen shook her head. "Nope, you go right ahead and have fun. You need to get away from this place every once in a while."

"Great! I think I'll see if Holly can come. I need to buy a present for Alex, and I can't do that with him there. I ordered something for Holly off the Internet and it's already here, so I don't have to worry about her."

Leslie stood and cleared her dishes, then went into the living room to call Holly.

"Oh, my God. You *still* haven't done your Christmas shopping? This is, like, a shopping emergency. Hold on, let me ask my mom." The line was silent for a few minutes before Holly came back on the line. "She said yes! How soon can you be here to pick me up?"

"Dad said we could leave here in half an hour, so probably about forty-five minutes."

"Great, that's just about enough time for me to get ready. See you then!"

Leslie chuckled as she hung up the phone. Her friend was much more concerned about her appearance than Leslie was, insisting on makeup and an outfit change for every outing. Dan had given Leslie permission to wear makeup when she started high school a few months before, but she rarely felt the need to wear more than lip gloss.

Leslie hurried upstairs to shower and change. It took some time to rifle through her closet to find something that would be acceptably fashionable enough to wear to the mall with Holly, but she was ready by the time Dan jingling his keys at the bottom of the stairs to indicate he was ready to go.

"Do you want to swing by the bank to pull some money out of your savings account?" he asked while they walked out to the car.

Leslie considered his question before answering, "Yes, I think that's a good idea. I can probably use my ATM card at most places, but some stores might only take cash."

The bank was not far out of their way, and they soon

pulled into Holly's driveway. Her house was large and stately, a two-story with eight columns in the front that soared from the front porch to the overhanging roof. The porch ran the length of the house, and garlands of pine boughs were wrapped around the rail at the front of it. The house was festooned with Christmas lights, wreaths and big red bows, and light sculptures of deer graced the massive front lawn. Leslie loved visiting the Moores' house at any time of year, but Christmastime was her favorite.

"Hello, Leslie," Holly's mother said when she opened the door. "It's so nice to see you! Come on in; Holly will be down in a minute. What a nice skirt you're wearing!"

"Thank you, Mrs. Moore," Leslie said, smoothing her denim skirt with her hands. It was the one she had purchased a few months before for her first date with Alex.

"So, do you have your list all ready? Do you know what you plan to buy?" Mrs. Moore inquired.

"I have some ideas, but I'll need to look around a bit before I know for sure."

Just then, Holly came down the stairs looking like she had stepped out of a fashion magazine. Leslie smiled to herself; Holly always looked nice at the barn, but she went all out when there weren't any horses around.

"Ready? Do you have enough money?" Mrs. Moore asked her daughter.

"Yeah, Mom, thanks. I've been saving."

Although the Moores had a lot of money, they expected their children to work for their allowance and privileges like horses. They were expected to keep a budget and manage their money sensibly.

"All right, then. You two have fun! Merry Christmas, Leslie!"

"Merry Christmas, Mrs. Moore!" Leslie led the way out to the car and they climbed in.

"You look very nice, Holly," Dan said. "I don't think I've ever seen you without riding clothes on."

Leslie rolled her eyes. "You have too. Dozens of times!"

"My mistake. You know us men; we never notice anything. At least, that's what Helen keeps telling me."

Leslie and Holly giggled. While Dan drove, the girls discussed which stores at the mall they should visit first. They finally decided to start at the end of the mall where the electronic store was and work their way through to the other end.

"Is there a particular time you need to be home, Holly?" Dan asked.

"Mom said I just need to be home for dinner at six o'clock," Holly answered.

"How about I plan to pick you up at five? That'll give you time to see a movie if you want. If you decide to come home before that, you can call."

"That sounds great!" the girls chorused, and then they giggled.

"Jinx!" they yelled in unison. They burst into giggles again.

"Here we are," Dan announced, pulling into the drop-off area at the north end of the mall. "The electronic store is inside to the left. I'll meet you at the south entrance at five unless you call me."

"Thanks, Dad. See ya!" Leslie started to climb out of the car, but Dan put out a hand to stop her.

"Don't leave the mall under any circumstances, unless it catches on fire or something, got it? I want you to stay there, where it's safe and I don't have to worry about you."

"Yes, Dad."

"And I know I can trust you two to behave like grown-up girls."

"Of course, Dad!" Leslie rolled her eyes. She couldn't remember the last time she had gotten in trouble for misbehaving.

"I know you're good girls with common sense, but I have to do the dad thing every once in a while, you know? While I'm at it, don't do drugs or drink alcohol. Did I leave anything out?"

Leslie smiled and reached over to give him a quick peck on the cheek.

"Got it, Dad. We'll be safe, we won't take candy from strangers, we won't do drugs and we won't steal or otherwise raise havoc." She used her index finger to draw an X on her chest. "Cross my heart."

"Thanks, Leslie. All right, you'd better get out; the guy behind me probably isn't too happy with us right now. Have fun!"

The girls scrambled out of the car and onto the sidewalk, slamming the car doors behind them.

"We're free at last!" Holly said.

"As long as we don't leave the mall, that is," Leslie said with a grin. "Now let's go get to it!"

They walked inside and quickly found the electronic store, where Leslie hoped to find something for Alex.

"He likes those little handheld electronic games," she told Holly.

After examining the many gadgets and toys in the store and exclaiming over the more elaborate ones, Leslie finally picked out a game she thought Alex would enjoy that was in her price range.

"Are you sure he doesn't have that one?" Holly asked.

"Pretty sure," Leslie answered. "I think I've seen all of the ones he has, and I don't remember seeing this one before. Besides, the sign says it's a new release."

Just to be safe, she asked for a gift receipt from the cashier when she went to the register to pay.

"That way he can exchange it if he needs to," she explained to Holly.

They left the store and looked around at the nearby stores. "Where should we go next?" Leslie asked.

Holly considered for a moment, and then said, "Let's go to that accessories store. I still need to get something for my sister."

They worked their way through the mall, browsing in the stores that interested them. Holly had finished most of her shopping, but she found a few things for herself and family and helped Leslie find items for the few people on her list. Leslie even managed to buy Holly a sparkly bangle bracelet in secret while Holly tried on clothes. By noon, they had reached the food court and finished shopping for everyone on their lists.

"Ready for lunch?" Holly asked. Her stomach rumbled in answer, loud enough for Leslie to hear.

"Definitely. Where do you want to eat?"

"How about the gyro place?"

Leslie giggled. "It's pronounced g'year-oh, not jy-roh!"

Holly slapped her arm playfully. "Whatever! Do you want to eat there or not?"

"Sure."

Over lunch, they decided to watch a movie at the discount movie theatre at the end of the mall. The theatre played movies that were old enough to be out of the regular theatres but not quite old enough to be sold on DVD. Holly looked up the show times using the Internet on her cell phone, and they selected a comedy that was starting in half an hour.

"Ugh, I'm so full," Holly said. "That gyro was huge."

"G'year-oh," Leslie reminded her, and Holly rolled her eyes. "Does that mean you don't want popcorn at the movie?"

"What? Of course I want popcorn. Popcorn doesn't count as food, silly."

"Gosh, I don't know what I was thinking!"

By the time the movie was over, both girls decided they had had enough of their outing and called Leslie's father to pick them up. They were tired of carrying their shopping bags, and they were tired of fighting their way through the holiday shopping crowd.

They sat on benches outside the south entrance of the mall and waited for Dan. "Whew, what a relief to put these bags down," Holly huffed. "I feel like my arms are going to fall off."

"Well, if you hadn't bought so many clothes for yourself, your bags wouldn't be so heavy," Leslie teased.

Holly stuck her tongue out in response.

Their ride arrived shortly and parked in the loading zone. Leslie gathered her bags and tried to hold them behind her while she walked toward the car. She had to set them down to open the door.

"No peeking, Dad!" she told him sternly. "Can you pop the trunk so I can put these in it?"

"Sure! Need some help?" he answered, winking.

"Ha ha. Nice try, but no."

Bags safely stowed, the girls climbed into the car and

Dan pulled away from the curb.

"So, did you have fun, girls?" Dan asked.

"Loads, Mr. Clark. Thanks so much for driving us," Holly answered.

"Yeah, thanks Dad," Leslie chimed in.

While he drove, the girls filled him in on the stores they visited, some of the things they bought, and the movie they watched. They talked all the way to Holly's house. When they arrived, Leslie helped her friend carry her purchases inside.

"Thanks again, Leslie," Holly said, hugging her goodbye. "I had a lot of fun. It was nice to see you outside of the barn and school for once."

Leslie laughed. "It doesn't happen very often any-more, does it? It was fun. Thanks for helping me pick stuff out."

They waved goodbye and Leslie went back to the car. On the way home, she fell silent. While she had been with Holly, she had forgotten all about her worries over Spark, but the thoughts crept back in when her friend was no longer distracting her.

It seems like this is all I've thought about for months, she pondered miserably. *When will it be over?*

Christmas morning was one of the best Leslie had had since her mother died. She woke up to the smell of coffee, hot chocolate, bacon and waffles. Leslie opened her eyes and took in a big whiff, then sighed.

It's Christmas morning, she reminded herself and she smiled. She stretched lazily and enjoyed the moment, then rose, put her slippers and robe on, and hurried down-stairs.

Dan was bustling around the kitchen when she walked in.

"Where's Mom?" she asked, trying to sneak a piece of bacon off a plate.

Dan playfully slapped her hand away. "She's out feeding, but she should be back in a few minutes. Can you help me carry everything into the dining room?"

"Sure," she said, picking up the plate of bacon and a pitcher of orange juice.

"Without snitching *anything* until your mom comes in?" he teased, eyes twinkling.

Leslie stuck her tongue out at him and walked out to the dining room with her burden. She helped her father to make sure the breakfast table looked perfect, and they were just finishing when Helen walked in, stomping her feet and rubbing her hands together.

"Merry Christmas!" she announced.

"Merry Christmas!" Dan and Leslie responded in unison, rushing to meet her at the door and wrap their arms around her in a group hug.

"Well, that's a pleasant way to warm up!"

"Thanks for feeding the horses, Mom," Leslie said, releasing her hold and helping Helen with her coat. "I would have helped you."

"I know, but I wanted you to sleep in and enjoy your morning. Now, let's get to eating that breakfast before it gets cold so we can open presents!"

They sat and dug into breakfast, relishing the sweet, crispy waffles and crunchy bacon. When the last bite had disappeared, Dan pushed himself away from the table and patted his stomach.

"Ah, that was good. You don't have to say it. I outdid myself. I know."

He winked, and the girls laughed.

"Now the question is, do we do dishes first, or open presents?"

"Presents!" Leslie exclaimed, at the same time Helen said, "Dishes!" and they all laughed again.

"Since the women of the house can't come to an agreement, I guess that means the man of the house has to decide," Dan said, grinning mischievously while he scratched his chin and pretended to consider the matter seriously. "On the one hand, Helen fed all the horses all by herself, so maybe she should get her way."

"Dad!"

"But on the other hand," he continued, "Christmas *is* all about presents."

"Dan!" Helen tried to sound stern, but the effect was ruined by the grin on her face.

"I have decided..." he paused dramatically, and Helen and Leslie made a show of sitting on the edges of their seats, each with her hands clasped.

"Presents!" All three leapt to their feet and cheered, laughing and racing each other to the living room with mugs in hand, where the Christmas tree guarded its booty.

They sat on the floor in front of the tree, Leslie and Dan in their pajamas, Helen in her jeans and long-sleeve shirt. Helen and Dan had opened their gifts to each other the night before while Leslie made herself scarce so they could have a romantic evening, so most of the remaining presents were for her. The little family sipped their warm drinks and enjoyed each other's company as much as they enjoyed the presents.

There were several small things, like a fun horsey t-shirt, a calendar with horses on it for her room, and new pajamas. After she thought she had opened everything, her father pulled a large, flat gift from behind the tree. She had not seen it sitting back there behind everything before.

Leslie pulled the paper off curiously, seeing a bit of picture frame and then a picture that revealed more of itself the more paper she pulled off. She saw her face with a top hat, followed by her saddle seat tuxedo and Lucky's head in a bridle. It was a painting that had been made from her win picture at Nationals earlier that year.

Leslie froze and stared at it. "It's—it's gorgeous. Just gorgeous!" Holding the painting with one hand, she hugged each of her parents in turn with her other. "It's the most perfect thing I could imagine. Thank you so much!"

"We thought you would enjoy having this to remember your experience by," Helen said, her eyes sparkling.

"But, how?" Leslie asked.

"We took the photo to an artist in town," Dan said. "And she painted it. Didn't she do a beautiful job?"

"It's amazing!"

They carried it upstairs, and Dan helped her hang it on her bedroom wall, across from her bed where she could see it when she woke up in the morning.

"It's perfect!" she announced, clapping her hands together.

"I'm glad you like it, honey," Dan said, squeezing her shoulders with one arm.

The three of them stood there for a moment, gazing at the portrait and remembering everything that happened that day and the days leading up to it.

Leslie came out of her reverie first. "Oh! We're not done opening presents. I need to give you yours!"

They trekked back down the stairs and reclaimed their positions by the tree. Leslie handed Helen her gift first, a fleece hoodie to keep her warm while she worked horses in the winter time. For her father, she had purchased a tie tack with a pretty stone in the center that looked almost like a marble with blue and white swirled together.

"It's beautiful, Leslie!" he said, holding up the tie tack to the light. "I'll be sure to wear it to work tomorrow. Blue is my favorite color, you know."

"I know, and mine too." She smiled, and they shared an affectionate look for a moment.

"OK, let's go clean up the breakfast dishes, and then we can go for our trail ride," Helen said, standing.

"Yeah, I don't want to miss lunch, so we'd better get the show on the road," Dan answered with a wink.

They made quick work of the clean-up chores, then bundled up in layers of long-sleeve shirts, sweatshirts, jackets, scarves and gloves. It was a merry trio that walked down to the barn a half-hour later, where the horses had already finished eating. Leslie tacked up Spark and Helen tacked up Fred, then they both tacked up one of the old school horses for Dan.

Dan did not ride often, but he had gone on a few trail rides in the past. The horse he was assigned, Turkey, was twenty-five years old and rarely moved out of a walk. He was mostly retired, except for the occasional outing. Despite the name, Dan felt safe on the old horse, and Helen trusted Turkey to take care of her new husband and keep him out of trouble.

Leslie loved riding when it was cold out. She sought warmth from her furry friend, giving him a hug whenever she felt chilled. She loved watching their breath puff out in white clouds, and the horses were always very fresh and spirited when it was cold out. Even Turkey had his ears pricked up and his head bobbed along merrily while he walked.

Dan had not been in the woods since the fire.

"I didn't realize just how bad it was out here," he said soberly. "I guess I should have, but since Green Meadow wasn't touched, it just never occurred to me how much damage there was to the forest."

"Sad, isn't it?" Leslie asked. "It used to be so pretty in here."

"It is sad, but it's all part of nature," Helen put in. "Things grow, a fire comes along to clean it out, and it all grows back eventually. In fact, sometimes it grows back even lusher than before. Look over there," she added, pointing to a patch of new grass. "It's already starting to grow back."

"At least there's an upside to the devastation," Dan said. "It's just sad that people like the Bakers lose so much in the process. It kind of makes you think, doesn't it? How lucky we were, and how we could have lost everything too, if your place wasn't designed and maintained well."

"Our place," Helen reminded him. "And yes. I am very thankful we didn't lose anything."

They rode along in somber silence for a few minutes before Leslie spoke up. "Hey, guys, it's Christmas! We shouldn't be thinking sad thoughts. Let's look forward to all the wonderful things coming to us in the New Year."

"Very mature of you, Leslie," Dan said, gazing at her with a proud smile, which she returned. "I, for one, am looking forward to our first full year together."

"I'm looking forward to the next show season," Helen

added. "Those three little girls are going to be really fun to show with..." her voice trailed off, and Leslie turned her tear-filled eyes to look at her stepmother.

There probably won't be a show season for me, she thought. *Not if someone claims Spark.* She couldn't find the strength to say it out loud, but she didn't have to.

"I'm sorry, Leslie. I shouldn't have mentioned it. Don't worry, even if someone comes to claim Spark, we'll think of something."

"It's OK, Helen, and I hope you're right. The thing is, I'm looking forward to watching those little girls show some more, even if I won't be in the ring too." She patted her horse's neck and told him, "I just hope you stick around with us to join in the fun, Spark."

A week after Christmas, the Clarks rang in the New Year. However, their joy from the holiday season did not last. On January second, a truck pulling a horse trailer drove up the driveway and parked in front of the barn at Green Meadow. Helen and Leslie were finishing up for the day, and they walked outside to find out who it was.

Two men stepped out of the truck.

"Can I help you?" Helen asked.

One of them men, wearing a suit and loafers that did not look like they spent much time in barns, stepped forward and handed a manila envelope to Helen.

"My name is Frederick Cavanaugh, Attorney at Law. Dr. Morrison here is my client, and we have a court order to confiscate a horse we understand you have been housing for a few months by the name of Sirius."

Chapter Fifteen:
Court Order

This was the moment Leslie had feared for months. She stared at the paperwork the attorney had handed them, but her vision was too blurred to read it. She had managed to make out "court order" at the top and that was all. Her breath came in gasps, and she mentally ordered herself to remain under control.

The other man spoke up. "I—I'm really sorry, Ms. Clark, but Mrs. Miller had a substantial bill with me when she passed away, and the only way for me to collect on it is to take Sirius."

His voice was soft and kind, and Leslie believed he truly felt badly about the situation.

She nodded numbly. She knew there was no fighting it; the veterinarian had a court order saying he was the rightful owner of Spark.

"Can—can I say goodbye to him, at least?" Leslie found it difficult to get the words out, and her voice sounded fragile to her own ears.

"Of course; take all the time you need," he answered. "When I heard you'd been taking care of him all this time, I was afraid you'd become attached. I wish there was another way, but I can't just turn my back on Mrs. Miller's debt."

"I understand," Leslie said in a small voice. "Just give me a few minutes, and I'll bring him out for you."

She turned and stumbled blindly into the barn and down the aisle to Spark's stall. He nickered at her, and she lost control of the tears she had been fighting back ever since Dr. Morrison and his lawyer had arrived. She stepped inside the stall and threw her arms around Spark's neck and bawled into his mane for several minutes.

She knew she had to bring herself under control, but she could not seem to manage it. It had been hard enough losing Lucky as a show horse, but having Spark to take his place had eased the sting. With Spark leaving, she would not have a horse to ride at all. She had grown to love Spark; they had been through so much together, and she did not know how she was going to live without him.

She was starting to regain control of her emotions when she heard Helen's voice behind her.

"Leslie?" Leslie turned to face her stepmother, trying in vain to wipe her tears away. Helen stood in the doorway of the stall, holding a halter and lead rope.

"Dr. Morrison brought his own halter and lead rope. Leslie, it's time. Would you like me to take Spark out for you?"

Leslie thought it over and decided she could not face Dr. Morrison and his lawyer, nor could she stand to load Spark in a trailer and watch him ride away.

She nodded. "Thanks, Mom."

She turned to Spark and looked him over one last time, planted a kiss on his nose and told him shakily, "Goodbye, Spark. Be a good boy."

She ran out of the stall, out the back door of the barn and did not stop running until she was in Lucky's pasture with her arms around his neck.

She did not know how long she stood there, but it was dark and cold when she felt a hand on her shoulder. She turned and saw Helen standing there with red-rimmed eyes.

"Oh, Mom," she said, releasing her arms from around her horse's neck to put them around her stepmother's. She'd cried herself out; there were no more tears.

Helen held her tightly. "I know, sweetie. I know this has been really hard on you. We'll see what we can do about it, all right? There may be some way to get him back, so don't lose hope."

Leslie sniffed and nodded. "Thanks, Mom, and thanks for taking him out to the trailer for me. I thought I could do it, but in the end I couldn't bear to watch him go. It was just too much."

"I thought that might be too hard, and that's why I offered. You did a wonderful job with Spark, and I'm sure he'll have a good life if we can't get him back."

"I'm sure you're right," Leslie said resignedly.

Helen released her hold and used her thumbs to wipe Leslie's face. "It's freezing out here. Are you ready to come inside? Your dad has dinner ready."

"I don't think I can eat anything, but thanks all the same." She stuck her hands in her pockets, suddenly aware of just how cold it was.

Helen looked at her sternly, looped her arm through Leslie's and gently guided her toward the gate. "You need to eat to keep up your strength, Leslie. It won't do you or anyone else any good if you don't take care of yourself."

Leslie sighed. "I guess you're right. I'll try to eat a little something."

However, she only managed to pick at her food that night, and it was days before she could sleep or eat well. She was despondent; unable to take an interest in anything or anyone. Alex and Holly tried to cheer her up in a number of ways, but nothing worked. She was heartbroken over her loss, and nothing but time could heal it.

A new semester had started at school, but Leslie hardly noticed. Even Kate's taunts had no effect on her; Leslie just walked around in a daze, oblivious to anyone around her. Her teachers noticed the change in her and tried to draw her out to talk about it, but she refused to discuss the reason for her depression.

No one can understand unless they've been through it, she thought sadly.

At first, Leslie couldn't bear to go to the barn to do her chores or work horses. Helen left her alone for the first two days, but on the third, she walked into Leslie's room and told her she needed to get back to work.

"Leslie, I know you're still upset about losing Spark, but it's time to get back to work," she said kindly, sitting on the bed and ruffling Leslie's hair. "You can't hide away from the world forever, and Alex and Julie have had to do your work for you. It's not fair to them, Leslie."

"I just don't know if I can do it," Leslie said, refusing to look at her stepmother. "How can I work those horses, knowing Lucky is lame and Spark is gone? How can I watch people take their riding lessons, when I can't ride?"

"I know it's hard, but I really think it's the best thing for you. Sitting around your room and moping will not bring Spark back, but getting back to work will take your mind off it."

"So I'm supposed to just go on about my business as if nothing ever happened?"

"Coming back to work does not mean you're pretending nothing ever happened. It just means you're living your life. These things happen, Leslie, and we can't just hide in our room every time they do."

Leslie heaved a big sigh. She knew Helen was right, but she found it difficult to make herself stand up and do what she knew needed to be done. She heard Helen rustling around the room, opening and closing dresser drawers. She felt something fall on the bed, and she lifted her head to look: jeans and a long-sleeve shirt. Barn clothes.

"That's as much as I can do for you, Leslie. The rest you have to do on your own." With that, Helen turned and walked out of the room.

Leslie sat up and stared at the clothes for a minute.

I guess it really won't be that bad, she thought. She stood up and got dressed, then walked down the stairs and out to the barn.

Helen was already in the indoor arena, riding a horse. She gave Leslie an approving nod and smile as she rode by. Leslie walked to the office and read the assignment board. She saw that she had two horses assigned to her to work. Both were babies that were learning to wear a halter and be led around. Leslie smiled; that was her favorite job.

Helen must have thought the babies would cheer me up, she thought. She retrieved a tiny halter and a long, soft cotton lead rope from the tack room and walked out to the paddock where the two weanlings lived.

She walked up to the first one, a bay filly named Lily, and stroked her neck. Lily nudged her, and Leslie scratched the little filly on the withers, chest, and behind the ears. The little horse ate it up, leaning into Leslie's hand and stretching her upper lip out as far as she could. Leslie could not help but smile, it was so cute.

"OK, Lily, shall we try wearing the halter?" Leslie deftly slipped the halter over the tiny muzzle and buckled it behind the ears before Lily could react, but as soon as it was on, the filly shook her head a couple of times in surprise. She stopped and turned her wide, curious eyes to Leslie, as though waiting for an explanation.

"What a big, brave girl! Very good, Lily." She reinforced the praise by stroking Lily on the neck and scratching her some more. "Let's try walking a bit now."

Leslie looped the rope around Lily's rear-end, holding it so she could put pressure on the filly from behind to push her forward and encourage her to walk.

"Walk, Lily," she said, gently but firmly. She clucked her tongue and pulled gently on the rope, and Lily leaned back into the unfamiliar pressure. Leslie repeated the command and pulled a little harder, making Lily take a tentative step forward.

"Good girl!" Leslie exclaimed, making a big fuss over the filly for doing as she was told, even thought it was only one step.

Leslie continued working with Lily in this way, telling her to walk and pulling on the butt rope when the young horse didn't respond. By the end of the session, Lily was walking beside Leslie with only a little bit of encouragement. Leslie was pleased with her accomplishment and moved on to Lily's paddock mate, a chestnut filly named Athena.

Athena proved to be a more difficult case than Lily. The chestnut filly was a strong-headed one and did not like to be told what to do. She leaned against the rope, kicked, bucked and did anything else she could think of to get out of doing what Leslie told her to do.

"This is why we usually teach you to lead when you're younger," Leslie told her exasperatedly, "when you're little enough to manhandle. It's unfortunate we didn't have time to work with you more then."

Leslie worked doggedly with the filly until she managed to get Athena to walk just one step when asked. She decided to take the small victory and call it a day.

Leslie sighed with relief and removed the halter, and Athena bolted away, bucking and leaping around the paddock to celebrate her freedom. Leslie shook her head and rolled her eyes at the filly's antics, then walked back into the barn to put the halter away and see if there was anything else she could help with.

Helen was standing at the pen board when Leslie came out of the tack room.

"That's the last horse," the trainer said, placing a check mark next to a horse's name. "We're done for the day. Thanks for working with Lily and Athena, Les. We let them go way too long." She sighed as she said the last part.

"You're welcome. They were fun, although Athena is going to be quite a handful!"

"I'm sorry I came down on you, Leslie, but it was time for you to start healing and living your life again."

Leslie nodded. "It's OK; you did what you had to do. I'm sorry I haven't been pulling my weight lately, and I promise I won't slack off again. Working with the babies made me realize just how much I love working with any horse, even if it isn't mine."

She sighed and shook her head. "I can't believe I acted so spoiled. After all, this time last year, I didn't even own a horse, and for a time, I had two."

"Atta girl, Leslie. It's nice to have you back." Helen smiled and reached one arm around Leslie's shoulders and gave them a squeeze. "And you do still have one horse, remember? Want to take a walk out to say hello before we go in to dinner?"

Leslie nodded. "That sounds like a wonderful idea. Let me just grab a carrot first."

She went into the lounge and retrieved a carrot out of the refrigerator, and then they walked out into the blustery cold together. When they reached the pasture, Lucky was grazing at the far end. Helen opened the gate so they could walk through and closed it behind them.

"Figures, he's at the other end of the pasture. It's like he wants to make things hard for us!" Leslie huffed.

Before they had gone more than a few feet, Lucky lifted his head and whinnied at them, then started to walk, then slowly trot toward them. Leslie stopped, stunned. Turning to look at Helen, she said, "He's trotting!"

Helen narrowed her eyes and watched Lucky critically.

"He is, but he's still off on that back leg. He may not be in pain anymore, but he still doesn't have full use of that leg."

She looked at Leslie and smiled reassuringly. "Definitely a good sign, though!"

A huge grin appeared on Leslie's face, and she broke into a brisk walk to meet Lucky partway. "Lucky, I'm so happy to see you feeling better!"

They met in the middle of the pasture, and Leslie hugged his neck tightly before giving him his carrot. He munched happily, pricking his ears and bobbing his head up and down before looking for more treats.

"What a nice surprise," Leslie continued, pushing his nose away from her pocket.

"Just don't overdo it, young man," Helen said, stroking the gelding's neck. "You still have a lot of healing to do."

Leslie gazed thoughtfully at Lucky for a few moments, enjoying his warmth and presence. "It is funny how horses that need help seem to find their way to me, isn't it?" she said.

Helen chuckled. "You do seem to have a knack for finding them. The nice thing is, the horses you find are diamonds in the rough."

"I do, huh? You know, I was thinking of something..."

"Yes?" Helen asked, looking at her curiously.

"What if I sort of kept looking for these diamonds in the rough and rehabilitating them and making them into show horses?"

The idea set Leslie's heart to pounding in excitement.

"Leslie, that's a wonderful idea, but there's just only so many horses we can afford to take care of, and we can only show so many horses ourselves."

"What if I found them, trained them, and sold them? We'd be doing something good for the horses that deserve a second chance, and it'll be fun."

Her eyes searched Helen's, beseeching her to understand what Leslie wanted to do.

Helen chuckled. "Sell them? After the way you got attached to Spark?"

Leslie's eyes slid to the side. "Well, OK, I did get pretty attached to him. But, if I get a horse knowing I'm going to turn around and sell him, I won't let myself get attached. I don't get too close to the horses that come in for training, do I? I'll just think of the rescue horses as training projects."

She looked back at her stepmother to look for her reaction.

Helen's eyes softened, and Leslie thought she might be relenting a little. "OK, but what if the horse doesn't sell? We'd be stuck with it."

"Well, yeah, I guess that could happen, but we'll be really selective about the ones we pick to make sure we'll be able to find them a home. We could sell them really cheap if we have to, and even if we don't make a profit, at least we saved a horse from neglect or the slaughter house. Please? We have lots of room here."

Helen looked around as if she wanted to verify Leslie's last statement, then back at Leslie. "I don't know, Leslie. Are you sure this is a good idea?"

"I really think I could make it work, and you and Julie and Alex will help if you need to, right? Think of all the great experience I would get, and all the horses we could save."

Leslie was determined. She had only thought of the idea a moment before, but the more she thought about it, the more she knew it was what she wanted to do—needed to do.

"Just one horse at a time. That's all I ask."

Helen looked at her for a moment, considering, while Leslie held her breath. Finally, Helen nodded. "OK, we can try getting *one* rescue horse to resell. I'll help you if you need it, and we can ask Alex and Julie, but it can't interfere with any of your other duties, do you understand?"

Leslie let her breath out as a grin split her face, and she nodded enthusiastically. "I understand! Oh, Mom. Thank you so much!"

She threw her arms around her stepmother, who returned the hug. Leslie's heart felt lighter than it had in weeks.

"I'll make it work, you'll see. This will be so much fun!"

They gave Lucky a final pat and walked together to the pasture gate, arm in arm. "Should we give a name to your little operation?"

"Yes, we should!" Leslie thought it over a moment, but her thoughts were interrupted when she was suddenly pushed from behind, causing Helen to let go of her arm. She stopped and turned around to see Lucky standing there behind her, ears pricked toward her.

"Oh, Lucky. You are so silly! It's lucky I rescued you, huh?"

She gave him an affectionate pat as she spoke.

"Leslie, that's perfect!" Helen exclaimed, clapping her hands together, eyes shining in delight.

Leslie stared back at her, perplexed. "What are you talking about? What's perfect?"

"The Lucky Horse Rescue!"

That night at dinner, Helen and Leslie explained to Dan what they wanted to do. He listened carefully, not interrupting or making jokes like he usually did. When they finished speaking, he nodded thoughtfully.

"Well, this sounds like a noble thing to do, if you can

help some horses in need. And it seems like you could make a little bit of money at it if you do it right. It's a little risky, though. Isn't it?" The last was directed to Helen.

"Anytime you do anything with horses, there's risk involved. The horse could turn up lame; it could have some kind of mental problem; you can get hurt. As long as we're really careful about the horses we take in to make sure they are horses we can place elsewhere, we should be fine. Even if we get stuck with an extra horse or two, it won't be too much more of an expense than the horses we're caring for now."

"Well, you know I respect your knowledge and experience, and you've done a great job running Green Meadow, so I know you have a good head for business on your shoulders. If you say you and Leslie can do this, I say go for it. I'll cheer you on."

He raised his water glass in a toast, and Leslie and Helen clinked their glasses against his.

"To the Lucky Horse Rescue!" he said, and two female voices echoed him.

After dinner, Leslie went into the living room to call Alex. "Hey, stranger," he said, "I haven't talked to you in days. Are you feeling better?"

"Yeah, lots. I was pretty upset and depressed for a while, but I think I'm coming out of it now."

She explained everything that had happened that day.

"Wow, you're starting your own horse rescue? That's huge!"

"I know, but it's only one horse at a time, at least for now. After all, I still have school, and I can't let my other duties at the barn suffer. Would you be willing to help me?"

"You bet! I'd love to."

They chatted for a few minutes more about the barn and school, then said good night and hung up. When Leslie went to bed later that night, she tossed and turned, unable to sleep. Her mind whirled with images of the horses she would find, of training and showing them and helping them find loving homes.

It was so late when she fell asleep that she nearly slept through the alarm the next morning. In fact, she would have slept through it if Helen had not banged on her door and woken her up.

"Leslie! If you don't hurry, you're going to miss the bus! Up and at 'em!"

Leslie groaned. She considered asking Helen to drive her so she could get a little extra sleep, but she immediately felt guilty. Helen had a lot of work to do, and taking an hour out of her day to drive Leslie to school would throw her schedule off for the whole day. Leslie tossed the covers aside and dragged herself out of bed, took the fastest shower of her life and dressed quickly. Helen was already out at the barn by the time Leslie got to the kitchen. She grabbed a toaster pastry out of the pantry and checked her watch; there was no time to heat it up, so she ate it cold while she dashed outside and down the driveway to the bus stop.

She arrived just as the bus was approaching, and she sighed in relief and climbed on board. Alex was waiting for her with a seat saved, and she flopped into it.

"Whew," she breathed. "I overslept and thought I was going to miss the bus! Thank goodness I made it."

"It's nice to see you too," Alex said, grinning.

Chapter Sixteen:
New Horse

It was Saturday morning two weeks later, and Leslie stretched lazily in bed for a few moments before getting up. Between working at the barn and going to school, she rarely had a day off, but she didn't mind. Her work at the barn was what she loved to do more than anything else in the world, and Saturday was her favorite day of the week, when she could spend all day there.

Helen taught a lot of lessons on Saturdays, leaving several of her training horses to Leslie and Alex to work. Leslie felt like a real horse trainer on Saturdays, like she knew she wanted to be when she grew up. She rose, dressed, and walked downstairs, where her father had breakfast waiting.

"Good morning, sunshine," he said, eyes twinkling. "Got anything special planned for today?"

"Every day that I get to work in the barn is special, Dad!" Leslie said with a smile.

"I'm glad to hear that, sweetheart. So, you're still enjoying your life here?"

Leslie's jaw dropped. "How could I not? I'm living a dream! I live with the horses, and I get to work with them every day. How can I not love it?"

Dan turned serious for a moment. "I just wanted to make sure, Leslie. I know this was a big change for you, what with me marrying Helen and us moving out of the home you'd lived in your whole life. I just want to make sure that I'm thinking of you and your needs every once in a while. You would tell me if you were unhappy, wouldn't you?"

Leslie held up two fingers of her right hand. "Scout's honor, Dad. I promise not to hold out on you again."

Dan laughed. "You're not a scout! How can you use scout's honor?"

Leslie giggled. "Well, equestrian's honor, then."

"I guess I'll have to accept that."

After breakfast, Leslie walked to the barn. Helen was doing some paperwork in the office when Leslie arrived.

"Morning, Mom," Leslie called to her through the door when she went to the pen board to see what the training assignments were for the day.

"Sleep well, Les?"

"I did, thanks." Leslie scanned the horses' names to see which ones she was working. "Hey, what's this new horse?"

Helen looked up from her desk, brows furrowed. "What new horse?"

"At the bottom of the list. In the horse's name box, it just says 'new horse'. My name is next to it, but it doesn't say what it is or what I'm supposed to do with it."

Helen stood up and walked around her desk to join Leslie at the board.

"What are you talking about? We don't have any new

horses." She looked at the board and said, "That's not my hand writing. I think it's Julie's. She went on an errand so she's not here to ask. I guess we can go find it and see if we can figure out what's going on."

"Why would she bring a new horse in without telling you?" Leslie asked. "That doesn't make sense."

Helen shook her head, frowning. "No, and it doesn't sound like her. She's very responsible and wouldn't do something like that. All new clients go through me; she knows that."

"Let's walk down the barn aisle and see if the new horse is in here," Leslie said.

They walked together, passing several residents of Green Meadow's barn.

"There's a horse in Spark's old stall," Leslie said, pointing. They walked to the stall and opened the door to get a better look.

Leslie stopped dead in her tracks. "It—it's Spark!"

Spark walked over to her and nudged her with his nose, but she was afraid to move, as though if she did, she would wake up and the dream would end. He nudged her again, and she knew he was really there.

"Spark!" she said again, flinging his arms around his neck and holding him tight. He nickered softly in her ear, and it was more beautiful than any music she had ever heard.

"I—I don't understand," Helen said behind her. "What's he doing here? How did this happen?"

"I don't know, but it's wonderful!" Leslie answered, voice muffled by Spark's mane. Her cheeks were wet with happy tears.

"Perhaps I can offer a little explanation."

Leslie let go of Spark's neck and turned to see Julie

standing outside the stall, along with Holly, Alex, and all of the other clients from the barn. All of them were smiling so big, Leslie thought their cheeks must be hurting as much as hers were.

Julie looked apologetically at Helen and explained, "I'm sorry I didn't tell you, but I kind of wanted to keep it a surprise, and I didn't know for sure if it would work out."

Helen laughed. "I don't mind at all! What a wonderful surprise—but you must tell us what's going on!"

"Well, Holly and Alex and I were talking last week, and they were saying how sad Leslie was over losing Spark, and how unfair it was that she had to give him up. I explained to them that while it would have been nice for Leslie to be able to keep him after all the time and effort she put into him, Dr. Morrison had a legitimate claim to him because Mrs. Miller owed him money."

"And that's when I said, well, why don't we see if we can pay him what Mrs. Miller owed in exchange for Spark, because after all, if that's the only reason he wanted him, maybe he would sell him, and maybe we could figure out a way to raise enough money if it wasn't too much," put in Holly, speaking so quickly in her excitement that she was breathless by the end.

"And so I went to pay a visit to Dr. Morrison to see how much the bill was," Julie said when Holly stopped for breath.

"And she was just finishing my lesson when she was getting ready to go," said a tall, thin woman named Kathleen, "and so I asked her where she was going. When she told me, I said I wanted to help, so I went with her."

Julie nodded. "So I went to see Dr. Morrison, and he said Mrs. Miller owed him a thousand dollars, and he hadn't really decided what to do about Spark yet. Well, I didn't think we could come up with that much, so I told him all about what Leslie had been through. He knew some of it, but he said it would be no more fair for him to not get his money than it was for Leslie to have to give up the horse. I told him I understood, but asked him if he would be willing to wait to sell Spark until we could see if we could raise the money. He said he would give us one week, and then he was taking the horse to the auction."

"So I got on the phone to all the clients to see who would be willing to chip in, and everyone said they would, not matter how much it cost!" Kathleen added.

"How could we not?" Cindy's mother said. "It was a small price to pay, knowing how happy it would make Leslie. She works so hard to make sure our horses are happy and looking great; she deserves this!"

They stopped talking and looked at Leslie, as though waiting for her reaction. Her heart filled so much in her chest that she thought it might burst. "I'm overwhelmed. I don't know what to say, except thank you! I don't know how I could ever repay you!"

"There's nothing to repay," said a stocky woman named Liz. "There were enough of us pitching in that it wasn't that big of an expense, and we wanted to do this for you. Besides, we talked him into coming down on the price, since he would never get a thousand dollars at an auction house. We don't want to hear anything about paying us back, do you hear?" She smiled while she spoke, although she was trying to look stern.

Leslie laughed. "Well, I guess that's that, then! Thank you again. This is just the most amazing thing."

Spark nudged her again and she hugged his head to her.

"You're not going anywhere for a long time, Spark. You're mine now! Even if I never have your papers, you're mine and no one can take you from me now."

"Oh, that's the other thing we should tell you," Julie said, holding out a manila envelope to Leslie.

Leslie took the envelope. "What is this?"

"Look inside," Julie said with a grin.

Leslie opened the envelope and pulled out several sheets of paper. The first was Spark's registration papers. Next was a bill of sale from Dr. Morrison, agreeing to turn over ownership of the horse to Leslie. Last was the court order granting ownership of Spark to Dr. Morrison.

"I talked to the registry, and that's everything you need to transfer Spark into your name," Julie explained.

"You thought of everything, didn't you?" Helen asked, shaking her head in amazement. "How did you accomplish all this without letting on?"

"I have my ways," Julie said, winking at her. "Plus, I had a little help. Holly called the registry to see what we needed to do to do the transfer, and Kathleen gathered the paperwork. It was a team effort!"

"Oh, my gosh. We have to tell Dad!"

"I'll go call him from the office phone and tell him to get down here," Helen said. "Why don't you tack up your new horse and take him for a spin? I'm sure he missed you, and Dan would probably love to see you ride."

"Mind if we watch?" Kathleen asked, eyes twinkling.

"Of course not, but first I have to hug each and every one of you!"

Leslie was instantly surrounded by her friends who had worked so hard to make her dream come true, and she had never felt more loved or grateful than she did at that moment.

Chapter Seventeen:
Show Season

It was dark when Leslie's alarm went off, but she did not groan and hide her head under the covers like she usually did. Instead, she was instantly out of bed, dressed and downstairs within five minutes. It was show day, the first time she would be showing Spark at a class A Arabian horse show.

She had sent his paperwork into the registry the very same day he had arrived back in the barn and nearly cried when she received the new copy in the mail with her name in the owner's section.

"You can finally stop worrying," her father had said. Even though Spark was safe in his stall at the barn, having the paper with her name on it as owner had finally made it feel real—and it was the last piece that she needed in order to be able to show her new horse at Arabian Horse Association approved shows, including regional and national championships.

Dan was shuffling around the kitchen when she bounced through the door. Leslie guessed the early hour was the reason for his lack of energy and slitted eyelids. She also figured Helen must already be out at the barn.

"Why do horse shows have to be so early?" he grumped. "Your first class isn't even until one o'clock."

Leslie giggled. "It's just one of those things."

She sat at the table and dug into the plate of pancakes her father had set there for her. After swallowing a couple of mouthfuls, she added, "We have to make sure the horses are fed and watered, and if they're dirty we have to clean them up. Then, Helen will want to school two of the horses before their classes this afternoon to make sure they're ready, because they were bad yesterday, and two others aren't showing so they have to be worked."

"Hmph," Dan answered while he puttered around cleaning up, but Leslie could see the sparkle in his eye that told her he was only teasing. However, she did suspect that he would go back to bed as soon as she left. The coffee pot was cold and empty, which supported her theory. She finished the last of her pancakes, downed her glass of juice and took her dishes to the sink.

"I'll put them in the dishwasher, Dad," she told him, planting a kiss on his cheek. "You go back to bed until a reasonable hour."

Dan looked out the window where the dark panes showed that the sun hadn't come up yet.

"Well, if you insist," he said, drawing out the first word. He gave her a peck on top of the head and added, "I'll come watch you ride later. Good luck if I don't get to talk to you before."

"Thanks, Dad," she answered while she rinsed her dishes and he retreated through the kitchen door.

Once she was finished, she went outside and walked quickly to the barn, wrapping her arms around herself to ward off the morning's chill. She found Helen in the tack room, picking up a couple of things they had forgotten when they had set up at the show the day before.

"I think that's everything," her stepmother said when she looked up and saw Leslie standing in the doorway. "Can you think of anything else we forgot?"

"I don't think so, but there's always something, isn't there?" Leslie answered with a giggle.

The sky was beginning to lighten when they walked out to the car, but Leslie barely noticed. All she could think about was Spark, and what he would be like in their class that afternoon. She thought back to the schooling show she had taken him to months before. He had been good, but she still barely knew him then. They had been working hard ever since he returned home, and she hoped it would pay off and he would perform well.

"You're quiet," Helen commented, pulling Leslie away from her thoughts. Leslie realized she hadn't seen any of the scenery while they drove. Looking out the window, she saw landmarks that told her they were not far from the show grounds.

"Sorry, I was just thinking about Spark and wondering how we'll do today."

"You've come a long way with him," Helen said. Leslie looked over at her and saw that she was smiling, with a touch of pride twinkling in her eye. "You've really grown in your training ability. I've hardly had to help you with him at all."

Leslie blushed and looked out the window again.

"Thanks. You've taught me a lot, even when you didn't know you were."

Helen laughed. "What's that supposed to mean?"

Leslie smiled. "I watch you a lot, you know. I have for years. Between chores, while I'm dumping the wheelbarrow, when I'm cooling out a horse—whenever I have a minute or two, I watch you ride or teach. That way, I'm still learning from you even when you're not actually teaching me."

She slid a glance back to her stepmother to see how she received the confession. The corners of Helen's mouth had stretched further into a bigger grin, and she was nodding.

"I always knew you were smart, Leslie, and this is just another example. I love how you take every opportunity to learn that you can. You still have a lot to learn, but you're definitely on your way to being a trainer."

Leslie's cheeks grew even hotter, and she didn't know how to respond.

"Thanks," she mumbled, feeling awkward.

Helen cleared her throat as she made the turn into the show grounds. "Anyway, Spark is going really well, and he's a really good boy. I think you have a good chance to get some nice ribbons today."

"You know, it's funny. I haven't really even thought of that. Ribbons would be nice, but I'm just glad to be showing my own horse again. After all Spark and I have gone through just to get here, I'm just happy we made it."

Helen pulled into a parking space behind the barn and they climbed out of the car. Juan was already there, throwing flakes of hay to the horses in their stalls. Alex was setting up the groom room for the day, making sure all the supplies they would need were ready. Leslie fell into the familiar horse show routine, helping Helen work horses. She was surprised when Holly arrived, carrying a white paper bag.

"I brought lunch for you guys," she announced, handing the bag to Leslie.

"Thanks! Lunch time already?" Leslie said, peeking inside the bag to see sandwiches from her favorite deli.

"Well, it's eleven o'clock, and since your class is at one, I figured you'd be eating early."

"This morning has just flown by. Thank you for the sandwich!"

Leslie gave her friend a hug, and just then Helen rode around the corner on the last horse of the morning to be worked.

"Look, Mom, Holly brought us sandwiches from the deli."

Juan walked up to take the horse from Helen, and Leslie handed him his sandwich.

"That was nice of you, Holly," the trainer said. "Let's sit down for a few minutes to eat, and then we need to start getting ready for classes this afternoon."

Holly had brought a sandwich for herself too, so Leslie called to Alex to join them and the four of them sat in their chairs in front of their barn to enjoy their lunch.

"Are you getting nervous, Leslie?" Holly asked.

Leslie shrugged. "Not really. I haven't even had time to think about it. I just want to get out there and enjoy myself and Spark."

Holly shook her head.

"If I were you, I'd be totally nervous. I mean, I'm nervous just thinking about it. Heck, I get nervous showing Sundance, and we've been showing together for*ever*. Man. I just can't believe you aren't nervous!" As was typical for Holly, she said it all in one breath, the words coming faster as she went along. Alex said nothing, but Leslie could see that he was trying not to laugh.

Leslie giggled and shrugged again. "I don't know. I guess if I really wanted to win, I might be nervous, but I just don't have any expectations for today. We'll just have to wait and see what happens."

Leslie gathered up the trash and threw it away. She retrieved Spark from his stall and put him in the cross ties so she could start getting him ready. She had plenty of time, so she enjoyed the process of grooming him without rushing. She picked out his tail one hair at a time with her fingers until it flowed full and lush behind him. She used the brush on his long, silky mane and tail.

"Your hair has really recovered since the fire," she told him. "Must be all the great vitamins and minerals Helen feeds you."

Alex walked into the groom room to see if she needed help when she was halfway through currying and brushing her horse's body. Looking at her watch, she realized she had taken longer than she realized.

"Actually, if you don't mind finishing getting him ready, I guess I'd better go get dressed."

Leslie handed her curry and brush to her boyfriend, gave him a quick kiss and walked out to go to the dressing room. Holly was already in there getting dressed, so they chatted while they dressed and helped each other with their hair.

Once they were both dressed in their saddle suits with the coats that draped elegantly to their knees, they rolled up their pant legs and appraised each other.

"Do my hair and makeup look all right?" Leslie asked before she stuck her derby on her head and pinned it in place.

Holly looked her over carefully. "You look great! Do I

look OK?"

"You look perfect, as always. Now, let's go get our horses!"

Leslie picked up her gloves and put them in her pocket. She grabbed a riding whip from the corner of the dressing room on the way out. Alex was still in the cross ties with Spark and was putting on his bridle. She stood there for a minute to admire her horse. Alex had made him sparkling clean and sprayed his body, mane and tail with a product to make them sparkle. Spark's hooves shone with polish, and his eyes and muzzle were shiny from the baby oil gel Alex had applied to highlight them. The bridle with the maroon browband was the perfect finishing touch.

"Thank you so much for getting him ready," Leslie said to Alex as she took the reins. "You did a great job, as always!"

He smiled and shrugged. "I guess you did a pretty good job teaching me."

He slipped out of the stall to bridle Sundance for Holly, and Leslie led Spark out of the stall and over to the mounting block. After making sure the girth was tight, she stepped in the stirrup and swung up into the saddle.

Helen appeared at her side, having been busy with the many tasks that demanded her attention at a horse show. She unrolled Leslie's pants and smoothed them down. Leslie admired how much longer her legs looked with her pants draping below her heels.

"Now just remember what you told me, Leslie," Helen said while she slipped a strap under Leslie's boot to keep the pants from riding up. "You just wanted to get out there and have fun with Spark. No pressure, right?"

Leslie smiled, partly at Helen's words, and partly because she truly didn't feel nervous or pressured. "Right!"

With that, she gathered her reins and asked Spark to walk. She rode him to the warm-up arena and watched the other riders around her while she rode, walking several feet from the rail so faster riders could pass her easily.

When she approached the end of the arena closest to the show ring, her heart tightened and her stomach clenched. Kate was sitting on a horse Leslie didn't recognize. She could only see them from the back, since Kate was facing the rail. However, by Kate's furious gestures and the crossed arms and dour expression of the groom she spoke to, Leslie could tell that her rival was up to her usual tricks of making everyone around her feel miserable.

Leslie chuckled and patted Spark on the neck.

"Be glad you've never had to know her, boy," she told him.

She saw Helen and Alex walk out to the middle of the arena, so she rode over to her to see if there were any instructions before she started warming up.

"Looks like Kate got another new horse," she said.

"What else is new?" Helen asked with a sarcastic smile. "That girl has gone through more horses than I can count. Every time she loses a class, she gets a new horse."

Alex's only response was to spit into the dirt. Leslie and Helen gave him dirty looks for being so crass, but he ignored them. Leslie was secretly thankful for his support, even if it was in a way she didn't approve of.

"I know. I couldn't believe she sold Charlie at Nationals after she lost. She didn't even wait until they got home," Leslie answered wistfully. She was thinking of Charlie, the horse she had once been hired to ride and entered her first horse show on before Kate bought him out from under her. She had been sad when she had to give up the horse, but the incident led to her buying Lucky, so she managed to get over it quickly.

"Enough gossiping," Helen said when Holly rode up to them on Sundance. "Time to get to work."

Helen gave the girls their instructions, then continued calling out orders while they trotted and cantered around her in the warm-up arena. Leslie noticed that Kate was still arguing, but that more people had joined in on the discussion. She guessed they were her latest trainer and staff. She put them out of her mind and concentrated on her horse and what Helen was saying to her.

She had just finished her warm up and loosened her reins to let Spark walk and relax when the gate steward announced over the loud speaker that the class before hers was lining up for their awards. She rode over to Helen and Alex and waited while they unwound the polo wraps from Spark's and Sundance's legs, brushed out their tails and wiped the dust from horse and rider with clean rags.

"Just make sure you don't use too much curb rein, Holly. You know he tends to get heavy on the forehand when you do that," Helen said, and Holly nodded in response.

Helen turned toward Leslie and added, "Don't let him get too fast at the trot. Slow down your own posting, and that will cause him to slow down and take bigger steps. Got it?"

Leslie nodded. "Got it."

"The gate is now open on class 173, Arabian English Pleasure, Junior Owner to Ride. Will you enter the arena please?"

Leslie leaned over to get a quick good luck kiss from

Alex, then gathered up her reins and took a deep breath.

"All right, girls, time to go. Have fun!" Helen called as Leslie and Holly rode toward the gate.

"Good luck!" Alex called, and Leslie saw him waving at them when she looked over her shoulder to smile in response.

There were several other riders waiting to go in the class, Kate among them. One at a time, they each picked up the trot and rode through the open gate. When it was Leslie's turn, she murmured, "Come on boy, let's do it!"

He broke into a lively trot, with his ears pricked cheerfully forward. Leslie's heart filled with joy, the corners of her mouth spread into a grin, and she rode through the gate.

About the Author

Jennifer Walker is a full-time free-lance writer, editor and novelist, and her work has appeared in several different magazines, like *Modern Arabian Horse* and *Horseman's News*, and the anthologies *Elements of the Soul* and *The Ultimate Horse Lover*.

While she grew up riding saddle seat and still loves it, her current love is dressage--which she is learning aboard her Arabian stallion, Capt Han Solo+.

Jennifer has several novels in various stages of production, including more of the Riders of Green Meadow series.

You can contact Jennifer at her website:
www.AuthorJennWalker.com